LENA & IVAR

VIKING GLORY BOOK FIVE

CELESTE BARCLAY

All rights reserved.

No part of this publication may be sold, copied, distributed, reproduced or transmitted in any form or by any means, mechanical or digital, including photocopying and recording or by any information storage and retrieval system without the prior written permission of both the publisher, Oliver Heber Books and the author, Celeste Barclay, except in the case of brief quotations embodied in critical articles and reviews.

PUBLISHER'S NOTE: This is a work of fiction. Names, characters, places, and incidents either are the product of the author's imagination or are used fictitiously. Any resemblance to actual persons, living or dead, business establishments, events, or locales is entirely coincidental.

Copyright © by Celeste Barclay.

0 9 8 7 6 5 4 3 2 1

Published by Oliver Heber Books

"The real lover is the man that can thrill you by kissing your forehead."
~ Marilyn Monroe~

Happy reading, y'all,

Celeste

SUBSCRIBE TO CELESTE'S NEWSLETTER

Subscribe to Celeste's bimonthly newsletter to receive exclusive insider perks.

Subscribe Now

VIKING GLORY

Leif
Freya
Tyra & Bjorn
Strian
Lena & Ivar

- Lena Tormudsdottir + Ivar Sorenson
  - Lorna Mackay + Rangvald Thorsson
- Leif Ivarsson + Freya Ivarsdottir
- Jan Tormudsson + Yrsa
- Erik Rangvaldson
- Signy Thorsdottir + Torbin
- Bjorn Jansson
- Vigo Arneson + Frida
- Sigrid Torbensdottir
- Tyra Vigosdottir
- Jorgen + Risten
- Eindride Magnusson + Brenna
- Gressa Jorgensdottir
- Strian Eindrideson

ONE

Ivar's eyes swept across the battlefield as the hair on the back of his neck caused his sweat-covered skin to prickle. He took in the overcast skies—skies that did not match the scorching sun the Norse warriors had experienced during these last weeks in the Mediterranean. The darkened skies matched his current mood as he panted, trying to slow the adrenaline coursing through him after his last engagement with their Arab enemies. He had just slayed an enormous dark-skinned man whose guttural Arab language was still foreign to Ivar Sorenson's Norse ears. As Ivar looked into the dead man's vacant eyes, he watched a crow's reflection fly overhead. Odin's messengers Hunnin and Munnin brought a cheer from Ivar's fellow Norse warriors, who celebrated their victory with praise to their gods. But Ivar could not be less interested in prayer as he once again scanned the fallen bodies and those still on their feet, looking for a particular blonde head with a face that possessed the deepest cobalt-blue eyes he had ever seen. Ivar's stomach clenched as he searched for Lena Tormudsdóttir.

"Lena? Lena!" Ivar called out as his heart began

to pound with fear unlike any he had experienced in the battle only moments earlier. "Lena!"

"Ivar?"

Ivar ran in the direction of the voice that he feared he would never hear again; it had never sounded sweeter. He wove through members of his clan and leaped over the bodies of fallen Arabs and Norsemen, pushing past a group of women to where Lena stood. Disregarding those around him, Ivar pulled Lena into his arms. After a brief glance to reassure himself that she was uninjured, he stroked her cheek and dove in for a searing kiss that brought conversations around them to an abrupt end.

Lena's toes curled within her boots. The feel of Ivar's body pressed against hers reminded her of their time spent coupling the night before. Her hands roamed over his back and shoulders as the tension eased with each of her caresses. The intensity of his kiss deepened as he groaned within her mouth, his tongue swirling and mating with hers, mimicking what they both longed to do with their bodies.

When they broke apart at last, their foreheads pressed together, Ivar smattered kisses on the tip of her nose as he cupped her jaw.

"You scared me," Ivar's hushed voice brushed warm air across Lena's face.

"You're scared of nothing, or so you told me," Lena brushed her lips against Ivar's.

"There is a first for everything. I couldn't find you."

"But you did. You're holding me now," Lena pressed another soft kiss to Ivar's mouth.

Ivar pulled back and swept Lena into his arms. He did not look back to see who snickered or tossed randy comments at his back, nor did he care that his father's commander, Magnus, was calling to him. Ivar carried Lena across the low grassy field to a copse of olive trees, cursing that their spindly branches would not give him the privacy that the fir trees in the Trondelag would offer. When they were a safe distance from the others, he placed Lena on her feet again and pulled her against him.

"Now I am holding you," Ivar's voice rumbled within his broad chest. "And I intend to hold you all through the night as I make love to you over and over until I am convinced you are safe and within my reach."

Lena's brow furrowed as she looked into Ivar's hazel eyes. She saw a tempest brewing unlike any she had seen before. She and Ivar had known each other their entire lives, having grown up together and trained together; they had started sharing their furs four years earlier. There was something different about the tension between them, something that was no longer merely physical.

"Ivar, what's wrong?"

Ivar's brows shot up before he once again stroked Lena's cheek, tucking hair behind her ears.

"Nothing is wrong. I was afraid when I couldn't find you, and now I'm not because you are here with me."

"We have fought plenty of battles over the years, and many since we began sleeping together, but you have never reacted like this. What happened?"

Ivar straightened and looked over Lena's head. While she was tall even by Norse standards, she still fit tucked beneath his chin when he held her as he had only moments ago. He pictured the fight he had narrowly won. The Arab had nearly severed Ivar's head from his shoulders with more than one swing of his sword, and it had taken every ounce of Ivar's remaining strength to fend off the giant. Ivar stood well over six feet tall, with broad shoulders and a well-muscled back that came from years of swinging a sword and an axe. He pushed himself to be the best among all of his father's warriors and was stronger than many of the tribesman by far. As the jarl's heir, Ivar bore the responsibility of being his clan's future leader. But even at Ivar's towering size, the Arab warrior had stood half a head taller and was significantly heavier, making his blows rattle Ivar's teeth. Ivar had been certain he would die during that battle until a whiff of Lena's scent, a combination of Norse lavender from the Trondelag and incense found in the land they now explored, filled his nostrils and created a fierce need. A need for her and a need to survive. That momentary reminder drove Ivar to fight until he was the victor and able to search for the woman he realized he could not live without.

"I nearly died."

Lena offered him the placating smile one might offer a child who said something inane.

"We've all nearly died. I nearly died more than once today. How is that any different from any other battle?"

"Don't say that." The hoarseness in Ivar's voice gave Lena pause. "Don't ever say that. You can't die."

Ivar pulled her against him and tucked her head under his chin as he stroked her hair. Lena paused before stroking her hand over his chest and curling her arm around his waist.

"Ivar, what's wrong? You're scaring me."

"I thought I would never see you again. First that I would die; then when I couldn't see you, I thought you might have---" He finished on a muffled sob.

It was Lena's turn to cup his face within her hands and run her thumbs over the bristled cheeks.

"I'm here with you now. And besides some cuts and scratches, we are both just as hale as we were before the battle. You're still scaring me."

"Lena, I love you."

Lena's eyes flared open as her heart thumped behind her ribs. She never thought to hear Ivar confess what she had felt in her heart for years. They had begun their physical relationship after a drunken feast, but it had quickly developed into companionship and fidelity, neither seeking the company of another. They spent most nights together, and they enjoyed their time spent with each other during the day. But Lena was not the daughter of a jarl, and that made her an unsuitable long-term match for Ivar. Though it was painful, she had assumed Ivar did not share her feelings, knowing their relationship had no chance of progressing beyond what it was now.

"Lena, I've always loved you. My heart has known it since we were children, even if my head wouldn't allow me to admit it. Something clicked into place today, and I refuse to ignore what's obvious. I love you."

"I love you, too," she murmured. "I always have, but I never believed you loved me."

"Why wouldn't I? You are the most special woman I have ever met. You are all the things a man hopes for. You are the most loveable woman I've ever met. I fear other men know that too, and one will catch your eye."

"What men?" Lena stretched onto her toes to swipe her tongue across the seam of Ivar's lips, demanding entrance that he was only too happy to offer.

"Say you're mine. That you will always be by my side," Ivar demanded with a gruffness Lena had never heard before.

She pulled away and shook her head as she swallowed the lump in her throat.

"Always? You realize there can't be an always between us. Are you asking me to one day go from being your companion to your concubine?"

"What?" Ivar shook his head, unable to follow her train of thought.

"You will marry one day, and it won't be to me. You would take me as your concubine, making any children I bore you bastards? Forcing me to give up a chance for a husband and a home of my own? Ivar, I love you, but you would sentence me to a life of longing for what I can't have. A life where you may warm my bed some nights, but another woman claims your home and her rights as your wife. I—I can't do that. Gods, that would kill me."

Lena pushed him away and looked around wildly her before running towards the others, leaving Ivar staring after her confused by her logic. He had intended on proposing, and instead, he stood wondering why Lena assumed he meant to make her a concubine.

"You're an ass."

Ivar spun around to see his best friend, Eindride, approaching him.

"You're an ass. I bet you probably intended to ask her to marry you, but that's because I probably would have bungled things just as badly. You will be a jarl one day. Your father is going to arrange your marriage, and it won't be to a girl from our homestead. Lena knows that all too well. She's been dreading the day Jarl Soren announces your betrothal. She can only hope to find a man to marry once you leave her. To be your concubine would make her the most hated woman in our village. There are plenty of women already spiteful that she is the only one who warms your bed."

"You make no sense. Why would anyone hate her if she has a position in my heart and my home?"

Eindride looked at his best friend and shook his mane of sun-bleached hair. He wondered how a man who was a brilliant strategist did not see how his current strategy would fail.

"What woman will want to arrive to marry a man already bedding the most beautiful woman in our village? What woman will want to be frú while having to accept that her husband is making love to a woman of common birth? Do you think any of our clanswomen will side with Lena once you're married? They would be fools to choose her over their future frú."

"I will convince my father that Lena is the best, the only, choice for me. She is more than a pretty face. She has the will and determination along with the sense to be a powerful helpmate to me and a leader for our village. She is already a natural leader among the shieldmaidens."

"But she brings no alliance. She brings little dowry. In your father's eyes, she brings nothing."

"But my happiness."

"And since when did that matter? You will rule this clan one day. Your happiness is nothing compared to the safety and prosperity of the entire homestead."

Ivar bit his tongue, as disagreeing with Eindride was pointless. His friend and the second-in-command of Ivar's division of warriors was correct. No one, especially his father, would consider his happiness as a factor when arranging a marriage. However, Ivar knew that a happy jarl made for a successful jarl. His grandfather had been devoted to his grandmother. They had an arranged marriage, but they had fallen in love, and their partnership made his clan prosperous after decades of struggle against neighbors. His father and mother also had an arranged marriage and barely tolerated being in the same longhouse, let alone the same room. Their discord affected the entire clan. The men sided with his father, and the women took his mother's side. It caused arguments within many families, and the unwillingness to forgive one another for causing the friction festered between his parents. The discord was well known among their allies and enemies, and their enemies often used it against them during raids. His parents had played him against one another throughout his childhood, and the moment Ivar was old enough he escaped to raid foreign lands. He captained their fleet each year and fled the moment the fjord thawed enough for the hulls of their longboats to cut through the ice.

"We both know that a happy home sets the tone for the entire clan. We already have alliances with the neighbors who matter." Ivar observed.

"And a few of them are excited to fight on our side." Eindride agreed.

"My mother and father have worked hard to keep those alliances despite how they bicker with each other."

"And it will be your doing that undoes that."

Ivar grumbled as he looked to where Lena now stood, talking to other shieldmaidens, her back to him.

"Ivar, you must realize your father will try to arrange a marriage with Inga Thorsdóttir. Her brother Rangvald will make a powerful ally when you and he inherit your jarldoms."

Ivar's stomach dropped. He knew Eindride was right, but he dreaded the notion of being married to Inga. She had an even more sour disposition than his own mother, and there was something that always put him on edge. He did not trust her the woman.

"Gods help me and us if that's true. That woman has an evil within her. I can't tell what it is, but I have a strong feeling that she will be our downfall or will be a catalyst to whoever tries to destroy us. I will not marry her."

"You more than likely will. Who are you to stand up to your father? Unless he dies before you wed, you have no say."

Ivar had no chance to respond, as a clap of thunder roared through the air and the clouds opened, dropping sheets of rain on the battlefield. The storm matched Ivar's mood, as though Thor read his mind.

TWO

Lena watched Ivar's approach as she pushed her sopping hair away from her eyes. She ran from Ivar because the pain of thinking of him with another woman, a wife, always stole her breath away. They avoided discussing the future with a tacit understanding that there was not one between them. Their relationship would run its course, and one day a bride would arrive for Ivar. As the former companion of the future jarl, Lena stood a strong chance of finding a husband when she was ready. No man would approach her now, but once Ivar moved on, she would be a desirable mate because of her looks and her former status. It did not mean the future was not a constant thought. She recognized that they were both of an age to marry, and she had heard the rumors that Jarl Soren had already been making inquiries with neighboring clans to find his son a bride.

Their conversation that day made Lena run from Ivar in part because it felt impossible to look at him as the pain ripped through her and in part because she was certain she would be ill. She had run to avoid heaving across his boots. The bile still rose in her throat each time his declaration of love echoed in her ears. She wanted to shake her head until the sound fell out, but she knew that was impossible. Instead it left her with the memory of how her heart had soared only to crash seconds later, and the relief —then the crushing regret—of confessing her own feelings.

She knew Ivar, and she knew their conversation was not over. He would try to convince her that he controlled their fate, but she knew he had no more say in the gods' plans than she did. Odin and Freya would decide who he should wed to maintain the power that their clan had built through bloodshed and hard work. She might be lucky if Freya remembered to look down upon her and offer her a future with another man. A man she was unable to picture and did not want.

"Lena," Ivar slowed his pace as though he were creeping towards an injured animal, and in that moment, Lena felt wild and trapped. "Lena, wait. Don't run from me again. We don't need to speak of what we already said. I would enjoy your company simply because I'm relieved we both survived."

Lena looked around as other warriors searched for the dead members of their clan. A funeral pyre was already being constructed, and in the distance, Lena saw where they would camp for the night. The day was not even halfway over, and there was plenty of work to do despite everyone's battle exhaustion.

"Help me then. I need to look for our women who traveled without family. I must make sure they died with their swords in their hands, and if not, you can help me find them and return them."

Ivar nodded, thinking Lena already demonstrated the duties of a frú. No one gave her those responsibilities. She assumed them, not because she presumed an elevated status as his companion, but because she was a natural leader to the other women. If only his father would acknowledge what others understood, and if only he would recognize that no one would be a greater helpmate than Lena. Inga certainly would not. She had never trained as a shieldmaiden and had no interest in doing so. Her parents pampered and spoiled her. He failed to see her journeying with him, nor could he imagine her leading a defense if their homestead was raided while he was away. He saw her cowering in fear and defeat. She would probably open the gates to the enemy to avoid being attacked. The only thing he pictured her defending was herself if any man tried to violate her. Granted, the moment she opened her mouth and her nasal tones seeped into a man's ears, he would gladly forgo rutting with her.

"Which direction do we start?" Ivar would follow Lena's directions and do what he could. He trusted her decisions implicitly, and he would complete any task if it kept him in Lena's company.

They spent the next several hours working with the other members of their clan as they sifted through the fallen bodies to find their fellow Norse warriors and searched for the lost weapons. Men and women carried the bodies to the funeral pyre, laying weapons against chests with arms crossed over them. They piled the bodies of the enemy as far from the camp as possible. They would leave them to the animals or any of their enemy who returned once they left in the morning.

Ivar and Lena stood together as the pyre burned and the Norse bid farewell to the fallen. Some would venture to Valhalla and others to Fólkvangr. Those that the Valkyries selected would feast with Odin in the Great Hall, and some would find peace with Freyja in her realm. The keening sounds of women's voices as they sang the songs of the dead filled the air as the rain continued as a drizzle. The somber and gray weather matched the crowd's mood. Sparks flew from the fire, and some parts blazed blue where the metal from the weapons melted. Ivar's fingers entwined with Lena's as he squeezed her hand. She had lost three cousins in that day's battle, and he offered his silent support as she said her goodbyes to family she had fought beside for a decade. Ivar had already lost both of his brothers the year before, and Lena drew strength from Ivar's shared understanding of her grief. Ivar was now his parents' only surviving child, and the future of their homestead rested on his shoulders, a duty of which his father never failed to remind him.

Lena's trembles turned into shivers as the temperature dropped and the moon rose. Ivar was not sure if Lena would acquiesce, but she allowed him to draw her into the circle of his arms.

"Come," he murmured near her ear.

Ivar led Lena to where he had laid their bedrolls earlier. He eased her to the ground and sought hot food for their supper. They ate in silence as Lena stared into the fire, her thoughts a jumble of grief, both for her family and for the future she would not have. Once they finished eating, Ivar took Lena's hand again and led her into the copse of trees.

"Let me ease your mind, if only for a little while," Ivar whispered.

Lena looked into the hazel eyes she knew so well and nodded. She longed for the escape only Ivar offered. They came of age together and were the other's first, and thus far, only lover. Once they moved past the initial awe and wonderment of joining, their coupling had the fierce need as it did from the very beginning, but they were slower, savoring each time together. Ivar had proven to be a giving and considerate lover, and Lena had proven adventurous and caring.

As Ivar brought Lena into the shelter of his arms,

he realized she was still shaken from the funeral, and worse, their conversation from the last time they stepped among the trees. He wanted to distract her from her troublesome thoughts and bring her what relief he could offer. He pressed his arousal against Lena's mound, scared that he would rush her but unable, and unwilling, to hide his need for her. His hands slid down to her bottom and cupped the soft globes. Lena tilted her hips forwards as she tried to get closer, her need matching his. Ivar maneuvered them until Lena's back pressed against a tree trunk. He slid his hand to cup her breast as he kneaded the supple flesh. Her mewls grew more needy as her fists clung to the front of his tunic. Ivar slid the tips of his fingers beneath the neckline of her vest until he cupped her warm skin. His own groans matching hers.

"I can't wait, Ivar. I need you too much." Lena's breathy whispers sounded desperate to her own ears.

"Neither can I." His own need filled Ivar's voice. "I'm going to make love to you over and over tonight, Lena. I can never get my fill."

A shiver coursed along Lena's spine hearing Ivar's mention of making love and her anticipation for their coupling. Her moans began as soft mewls but intensified as her body reacted to Ivar's hands cupping her backside. The sensation of his hands kneading her flesh had her rocking her hips in a way that only instinct guided. She shifted in frustration as her body yearned for more, her sheath begging for their bodies to join. Ivar's responding groan as her mons brushed against his rod only increased her desire.

When Lena's cool fingers ran along his neck up to his cheek before cradling his jaw, Ivar was sure he would spend himself if he did not position them where it was possible for him to undress and sink into her. He pulled away and looked around the trees until he found a spot where leaves had gathered to soften the ground, but the overhead coverage kept the moisture from them. He took Lena's hand and led her to the spot where they stood facing one another. He pressed her palm against his cock as his eyes drifted closed.

Lena's impatience grew knowing that despite Ivar's pledge, they would not have the entire night together. She pulled at the belt that held his sword and laid it on the ground as Ivar did the same to her. She tugged at the laces of his leather pants, frustrated that they would not give with her first yank. When his rod sprung free, she gasped then licked her lips, still taken by surprise at the length and girth of his rod. Ivar's groan was one of agony as he watched a seductress emerge from his trusted shieldmaiden. Ivar lifted Lena off her feet and guided her legs to wrap around him. Her moan of unspent need as his cock pressed against her entrance had Ivar sinking to the ground.

As he pressed his length against her entrance, Lena rocked her hips in a timeless invitation. Her knees cradled his hips until she let them fall wide, and her hands sought the chiseled flesh of his backside. She marveled at how different Ivar's body was from her own. Despite their countless times together, his impressive physique still made her heart race. She wanted to remind herself of every inch of him, but her mind stalled when Ivar's finger slid along the swollen skin of her nether lips. A moan escaped before she stifled it, but Ivar's responding growl reminded her that he enjoyed knowing he aroused her. As he dipped a finger into her dewy sheath, she rocked her hips again.

Ivar pressed his finger into her, and her shudder of longing and her nails biting into his back told him she was ready for more. He slid a second finger into her and began to work her heated flesh. He stretched her as he stroked her inner walls, and his thumb found the hidden pearl that would push her over the edge. She grasped his face and lifted hers to bring their mouths together. She pressed her tongue against his lips, inviting his tongue to duel with hers. They went back and forth, each giving and taking.

Lena experienced a tightening low in her belly as a wave of sensation built. When it cascaded throughout her, and she moaned her first release, Ivar withdrew his fingers and surged forward, impaling her with his length. Their bodies moved together with a familiarity born from sharing their love and bodies for four years. There was no future to think about, only the present, as they both crested and crashed over the edge. Ivar groaned as the jets of his seed filled Lena and thanked the goddess Freya once more that Lena used pennyroyal to prevent pregnancy and to allow him to climax while they were still one.

They held one another, still joined, until Ivar's body no longer cooperated with his mind or his heart. He rolled to Lena's side and pulled her body flush to his. She wiggled until she pressed as close to him as they had been only minutes ago, but this time for comfort rather than for release. Ivar stroked Lena's hair, trying to relieve some of her tension, but her body was coiled tight despite the boneless sensation of only moments ago.

"I dread telling my aunt and uncle that all three of their children are but spirits now. It will devastate them."

"You don't have to do it alone, or I'll go to them instead."

Lena's fingers ran over the warm skin of Ivar's

chest as he held her. She felt protected from the outside world, but it was not enough to ease her mind.

"I must be the one. I promised to watch over them, just as they had promised to watch over me. I failed them."

"Lena, you and I both know that's not true. And your aunt and uncle understand what a battle is like. Your uncle has fought in them, and your aunt has seen the outcome. There is no way to watch over anyone other than the person who fights alongside you." Ivar drew a ragged breath as he thought of searching for Lena earlier. "Even I lost track of you, and we began the battle together." A tremor raced through Ivar as his body confessed his fear.

Lena came up on her elbow as she cupped Ivar's jaw. "Ivar, you know that wasn't your fault, don't you?" It had terrified her when she could not spot Ivar as the fighting drew them further apart. They had fought alongside one another for years. Eindride fought at Ivar's back while Lena and at least one other shieldmaiden fought along their flanks. The Arabs were skilled in drawing them apart and forcing each Norse warrior to fight a singular opponent, their strength in numbers evaporating. Her terror was not in fighting alone and dying; the terror came from not knowing where Ivar was and not protecting him. They had fought in that pattern since their first voyage together. They began sailing to foreign lands, along with Eindride and their other close friend Vigo Arneson, when they were sixteen. That was only four years earlier, but they had trained and fought close to home since they were children. Raids had necessitated it.

But once they began sailing to further afield to explore and invade, Lena, Ivar, Vigo, and Eindride were a force few could approach. Einar, Eindride's younger brother, joined them for the first time on this voyage. Eindride had been keeping an eye on Einar, and that was part of the reason he became separated from Ivar. Lena was pulled into a fight when she defended a fellow shieldmaiden who was being overpowered. There had been no way for Lena and Ivar to remain near each other if they both wanted to stay alive and do their duty to their fellow warriors.

"Ivar, you know that wasn't your fault, don't you?" Lena came up on her elbow as she cupped Ivar's jaw. "I was just as worried when I couldn't find you as you were. I hate that feeling."

Ivar drew Lena across his chest as she shuddered at her final thought. He drew a line along her collarbone with his kisses before he traveled the distance to just behind her ear. Lena's hand searched along Ivar's long body until she found his semi-aroused cock. She wrapped her hand around him and stroked as their mouths found one another, their kiss deep and sensual. Ivar lifted her, so Lena took his sword into her sheath. She pulled at his shoulders until he lifted his body to press against hers.

They sat, joined, for a long moment just enjoying the connection. Ivar lifted and lowered Lena as her inner muscles clung to his cock. His body cried out for him to stop talking and make love to her. Fire fueled their kiss, and the time for talking had ended. Their motionless joining had been a fusion of their souls as much as their movements now were a fusion of their hearts. They moved together until they both found their release, tumbling into bliss together.

Once again, Ivar positioned Lena against him, and she was content to burrow into his warmth. He drew their cloaks over them as their sweat-dampened skin began to cool. The air was pleasant, but he would also shield Lena's body from anyone's eyes who might approach. As they had on their previous journeys, Ivar held Lena while he took the first watch. In a few hours, he would wake her to make love again before she took over the watch, and he slept. Before the sun rose, they would rejoin their camp, acting as though they and several other couples had not crept away for privacy. No one dared to travel further than the safety of the camp, but many preferred to make their bed where others were unable to watch.

THREE

"We have been gone long enough," Ivar declared as his warriors crowded around him. "We sail for home!"

The crowd cheered as many breathed a silent breath of relief. Their voyage was a success. While traveling, they had swept through villages where they were greeted by people unlike any they had seen before. Used to finding men and women who looked similar to them when they raided England and Francia, they were unprepared for the olive-skinned, almond-eyed people of North Africa. More than one man found a woman to claim and return with, ensuring they had a bed slave to keep them company once they arrived in their perpetually frozen homeland. Once they tired of these thralls, most likely by the following summer, they would sell them to a slave trader. If the women were lucky, they might return to their homeland.

"Gather what we took yesterday, and we make our way to our ships. The gods are with us, and so are the tides." Eindride called out as Ivar and Lena faced the shore, ready to lead their people back to the longboats moored a few miles away.

The crews were quick to store their bounty beneath the boards of the deck in the shallow hulls of the longboats. Ivar, Eindride, and Vigo captained their own boats along with the seven others. They were a fleet of ten ships with dragons carved on their prows and large billowing sails on their masts. The fleet was impressive, and Ivar had insisted that they travel with nine as fortune smiled upon that number. He had predicted accurately; their pillaged goods were the greatest value ever collected.

The journey was long and arduous for all the Norse warriors, with the blazing sun shining overhead day after day. They had to go ashore along the way to collect fresh water and forage or hunt for food. There was only so much pickled herring that any of them wanted to eat. The coast of Spain proved a treasure trove, with a round orange fruit that was juicy and sweet, a treat none of the Norse sailors had ever enjoyed before. They found more of the round, deep red ovals that were salty and tangy, but they had already enjoyed those during their various stops along the North African coast. Oranges and olives became food staples along with dried beef and pickled herring.

Ivar and Lena took turns at the oars, but Ivar spent most of his time at the tiller. When she was not rowing, Lena ensured each crew member had their daily ration of food and warm clothing. They caught strong winds as they made their way along the coast of Francia, and then the British Isles. The crossing of the North Sea to their homeland was choppy despite a lack of wind and strong sunlight.

Relief surged through Ivar, as it always did whenever he arrived at his homestead. He helped Lena down from the boat, and they walked arm-in-arm along the dock until they reached Ivar's parents. Soren's scowl at Lena made Ivar protective. His heart seemed to skin and race at the same time, as intuition told him he would not like the news from while he was away.

Ivar's mother, Disa, stepped forward to embrace her son while casting a warm smile towards Lena. Disa may have despised being married to Soren, but she loved her son. She wished she were able to allow Ivar and Lena to marry. She would have her son find the joy in marriage that was lacking in her own.

"I see the voyage exceeded my expectations. The men are already carrying chests of riches ashore. Wherever shall we keep it all?" Soren chuckled, but the sound lacked any trace of mirth.

Ivar ground his teeth at his father's patronizing tone. If the man had not been his father and his jarl, he would have grunted and pushed past him. He wanted nothing more than to take Lena to his chamber for a hot bath, where he would scrub away the grime and salt encrusted to him and then make love to her after weeks of forced celibacy. His father had other plans.

"Rangvald and Thor are here."

Ivar did not dare cringe before his father, but he suspected why their neighbors were there. He felt Lena go rigid, as he still had an arm wrapped around her. She stepped to his side and bowed to Ivar's parents before darting away. Ivar returned his father's scowl as he made to follow Lena, but Soren grasped his arm.

"Leave your concubine alone while our guests are here. They will not want to leave Inga here if it's obvious your cock is plowing another field," Soren's voice hissed in Ivar's ear.

"She is not my concubine, and you know it. She is my companion and a free woman. You should feed them, then show them the gate. That would keep them from seeing what we can't and won't hide." Ivar bit out as he watched Lena reunite with her aunt and uncle. He had promised to be by her side when she informed them of their children's death. Instead, Lena was facing it alone. He ripped his arm away and looked down at his father, having grown several inches taller than the older man by the time he was fourteen. "I have a promise I must keep."

Ivar jogged away, wishing his father had been more circumspect, but knowing it was his intention to hurt both him and Lena. He arrived at her side just as her aunt began to wail, and her uncle pointed an accusing finger. Ivar stepped in front of Lena, and his thunderous look was enough for the older couple to turn away.

"Are you all right?" Ivar whispered.

Lena nodded her head, but Ivar was far from convinced. He took her hand and followed the path to the bathhouse, his chamber no longer an option after his reunion with his father. He realized they would not be alone, and he accepted he would have to wait his turn since the women would go first, but he could at least accompany her and be there when she finished. He would postpone his bath if it meant Lena was well cared for.

Lena stepped into the warmth of the steamy bathhouse and began to strip her clothes from her dirty and exhausted body. She was in no mood to talk to anyone. She had already spent months with the other shieldmaidens, and she was not in the mood to regale anyone who remained at the homestead with stories of sailing the high seas and battling foreign enemies. Lena just wanted to soak in the hot water and forget about everyone else.

"I see my husband and his whore have returned." A nasal and rasping voice grated against Lena's patience. Lena was not surprised by who she found on one bench that surrounded tubs already filled with other women. All conversations ceased as the women awaited Lena's response. She had no intention of giving one.

Lena stepped into a tub that a thrall had already filled and slid under the water, letting it wash over her and cover her tangled hair. She opened her eyes when she sensed someone had stepped near her tub. The form of a woman stood askew beside the lip of the tub, and as Lena pushed along the bottom to sit up, a hand reached down. The hand grasped Lena's hair and pushed with more force than Lena expected. Rather than panic, Lena was still until the pressure eased, then she made her move. She was out of the water and onto the floor before anyone predicted she would flip her attacker over her shoulder and into the tub.

As the woman emerged spluttering and swearing, Lena stepped into another tub and wasted no time scrubbing her body. Inga stood in the tub with clothes stuck to her and dripping onto the floor.

"You shall pay for that, whore."

"Inga, sit down. There is nothing to pay from me, but you attacked a free woman. I am no thrall. You have no right to touch me unless you intend to fight me. We both know who the victor will be." Lena's tones were even and low as she scrubbed her hair. She finished with hushed tones, "I'm no one's whore, and you have no husband."

Inga was not finished lashing out at Lena.

"I do have a husband, as my father and Jarl Ivar have already signed the papers. We are wed but for the blessing."

Lena's heart lurched, but she forced her face to remain passive. She poured fresh water over her head from the urn next to the tub. When she stood, she allowed Inga to finally gaze upon her figure. She was lithe where Inga was stocky. She was tall where Inga was short. She was agile where Inga was sluggish. Lena intended to show Inga what Ivar had already proved he preferred. Inga gasped, her face going from scarlet to ashen in a matter of heartbeats. Lena walked towards Inga and leaned sideways to whisper in Inga's ear.

"I would eat a few less sweets, so Ivar can find your sheath; otherwise, his sword will continue to find mine."

Lena wrapped a drying linen around her and pulled the bathhouse door open, caring little that she was about to walk across the homestead virtually naked.

FOUR

Ivar looked up to see Rangvald Thorsson and Signy Thorsdóttir running towards him. He and Rangvald were the same age, and he liked the other young man. His sister Signy was beautiful, but her uncanny gift of second sight frightened him a little.

"She's in there!" Rangvald called as he and his sister came to a halt before him. "Inga."

Ivar's eyes opened wide as Signy made to push open the door, but stumbled as a woman yanked it open. Ivar turned to see Lena stepping outside with only a drying linen wrapped around her.

"Hello, Rangvald. Signy." Lena greeted them with a warm smile, but it faded. She stepped away from the others and flung over her shoulder, "Your wife is awaiting you."

Ivar glared at Rangvald before reaching for Lena.

"That's why we were running," Rangvald panted.

Ivar did not hesitate to sweep Lena into his arms then march to her longhouse. He pushed his way into the house before kicking the door shut. He deposited Lena on the ground and pursed his lips into a scowl when she glowered at him. Lena spun around and approached an older woman sitting beside the fire.

"Amma, you look well," Lena greeted her grandmother with a kiss on her cheek.

"Lena, *elskan min*, you are home."

Lena's heart swelled whenever her grandmother called her "my darling." It reminded her of her mother, who died giving birth to Lena's younger brother when she was four. It was one of the few memories she had left.

"I am, Amma." Lena looked into the clouded eyes as her grandmother's gnarled hands ran over her face and shoulders.

"You're soaking wet! Ivar, why are you letting my granddaughter walk around with sopping wet hair?" Her grandmother gasped when she touched the drying linen wrapped around Lena's body. "And without clothes?"

"That is why I brought her directly home, Amma." Lena's grandmother invited him to call her by the term of affection soon after they began their relationship. He had known the woman his entire life, and she was like a grandmother to him. It was not a stretch for him to think of her as such. However, knowing Inga was within the gates gave him a sickening feeling. He would lose the privilege of being part of Lena's family the moment he married Inga. He glanced up at Lena and feared that moment had already come.

"I didn't take any clean clothes into the bathhouse with me." Lena tried to soften her tone for her grandmother's sake, but she was still fuming.

"I may be blind, child, but I am not dumb. Something has caused a rift between you two, and I would imagine it comes in the package of a spoiled jarl's daughter who wants what isn't hers."

Lena shrugged, then remembered her grandmother was unable to see her.

"I had an encounter with Ivar's wife, and it was not pleasant."

"Stop calling her that. She is *not* my wife." Ivar crossed the room in a few long strides and took Lena into his arms.

"But she is. She told me your father and hers have signed the papers. All you need is the blessing."

"That's not true. If it were, my father would have been crowing about it before we even stepped on the deck. She said it to hurt you." Lena nodded and tried to pull away, but Ivar did not loosen his hold. "What else did she say, Lena?"

Lena bit her lower lip and shook her head before tilting it towards her grandmother.

"That was all I remember. I'm getting cold. I should get dressed."

"I'm sure her fingers are too cold for buttons, Ivar. She could use help, and my old fingers work about as well as my eyes."

Ivar grinned before stepping away and dropping a kiss on Amma's cheek. Once they were in Lena's chamber with the door closed, they came together in a heated kiss that pushed everything else from their minds, their need to reunite their bodies too powerful to ignore. Ivar ripped the towel from Lena's body, and his hands roamed over Lena's body as she began unfastening as much of Ivar's clothing as she could.

"Let me watch," Ivar's voice was hoarse with need.

Lena ran her hands over her breasts and belly until she reached the thatch of hair at the apex of her thighs. One hand skimmed back up to knead her breast and tweak her nipple as fingers from her other hand delved into her sheath and rubbed the pearl of her arousal. Ivar's eyes devoured the sight as he rushed to pull off his clothes. Once he was bare too, he reached for Lena's hand and brought the dew-covered fingers to his lips. He licked each one clean before sucking her forefinger into his mouth.

"I shall make love to you every way I can think of with my mouth and my rod." Ivar's hands squeezed the supple flesh of her backside before lifting her to wrap her legs around his waist. The tip of his cock grazed her entrance, and she shifted, trying to take him into her aching body. "Oh no, not yet."

"Ivar," she pleaded.

"I intend to enjoy every course of this meal." Ivar sat on the bed then laid back, pulling Lena to hover over his mouth. His fingers bit into her hips as he pressed her down to meet his questing tongue. Lena's moan filled the room as her head fell back, wet hair brushing against Ivar's thigh. Lena's hips undulated as Ivar flicked his tongue over her heated bud before sucking the sensitive flesh into his mouth. He raked his teeth across it before delving his tongue into her core.

"Ivar, I want you, too. Please. I need--" Lena's voice trailed off as mewls of desperation overtook her moans of pleasure.

"Greedy little thing, aren't you? Very well. I can't say that I don't long for you to run your tongue and satiny mouth over my cock."

Lena twisted around until she leaned over Ivar's steel length. She wrapped her hand around it and stroked it several times while Ivar pulled her hips back towards him and resumed his feast. She licked the tip, and Ivar's responding growl made her core vibrate with need. Lena sank her mouth onto his cock and tightened her lips around his swollen rod. Her head bobbed as his cock twitched. Their need matched one another as they both sought to give and take pleasure from one another.

"Enough," Ivar hissed as his body sped too quickly towards completion. Lena was not in agreement, sucking harder and faster, wanting to pleasure Ivar. An echoing smack landed across her backside, and Lena wiggled her hips toward Ivar. It was only a moment later that Lena felt herself flying as Ivar lifted her away and turned her to land on the bed with his body covering her. In the next instant, Ivar was buried to the hilt as his cock felt like it had come home. "You don't listen very well, do you?"

"Perhaps a spanking would make me pay better attention to your commands," Lena purred.

"We shall see about that after we have gotten our fill of one another."

"I will never get my fill. I will always want more." Lena snapped her mouth shut as her own words filtered through her mind.

Ivar's responding grunt and increased speed as he thrust into her had her arching off the bed.

"You will always get more. Lena, I will make you come day after day, night after night until the gods take me away. Then I shall find you in the afterlife and pleasure you there. You are mine."

Ivar punctuated the last three words with thrusts that verged on pain for Lena, but they only made her grow wilder.

"I am yours. Always. Do with me whatever you want. I'll never turn you away."

"You shouldn't have said that because when I'm done making love to you, I'm going to fuck you."

"That's what I want. What I need."

Ivar's kiss was savage and possessive, and Lena's matched him as they sought to prove their claim on one another. Lena sensed the tightening within her belly as she ground her mound against Ivar. The pleasure built into an inferno before exploding throughout. Her core squeezed Ivar's cock until he, too, exploded. Their kisses shifted from demanding to affectionate as they shifted from blind need to bliss. Ivar held Lena as he feathered kisses across her cheeks and along her neck.

"I love you, Lena." Ivar saw the flash of joy before sadness settled in Lena's eyes. "I will tell you that every day for the rest of our lives. I will tell you that before our families and our people. You are the one I will marry, even if that means we must run away."

Lena brushed the hair back from Ivar's face before twirling a lock around her finger. She tugged, and Ivar leaned forward for a tender kiss that made Lena sigh.

"I'm serious. I won't marry anyone other than you. Neither my father nor any other man can force me to make a vow I refuse to keep. My father would not make me an oath breaker and that is what I would be if I married another woman. I would never touch her. I would never live with her as a husband. I don't think even my father would want to shame a woman in such a way. I will not give you up."

"Ivar, we aren't children anymore. You can't hold on to me like a toy you won't share, and you cannot have a fit because your father tells you to do something you don't want to do. You have a duty to our people. That duty doesn't include me."

"But it should. Only a fool would think you aren't the woman best suited to be the future frú of this clan. My mother knows it, even if my father refuses to consider it. My mother has been guiding you and training you for years, before we even began sharing our furs."

"But I would bring nothing to our marriage but the clothes on my back."

"Which I would quickly strip you of." An irrepressible smile tugged at the corner of his mouth, making him even more desirable. He was already the most handsome man Lena had ever seen, but when he shared that smile that only appeared for her, she was ready to melt.

"Ivar, be serious." Lena had to look away as his smile was too captivating. "If the papers have already been signed, or even just drafted, then this marriage is moving forward. And it won't be between you and me."

"Why are you so ready to give up? Why won't you fight for us?"

Lena pushed against Ivar's shoulder until he rolled to his side.

"Give up? Give up? If I was ready to give up, do you think I would be here, making love to you and breaking my own heart? What do you think your father would do to me if I argued with him in public against this marriage? I would be dead before you even discovered his guards took me." Lena shook her head. "I haven't given up, but I also know dead warriors don't fight."

"I would lay down my life for you."

Lena gasped and her hands balled into fists. "Are you implying I wouldn't do the same? How many times have I risked my life to save yours? Just as many times as you have done the same for me."

"I meant I will die fighting to have you."

Lena shook her head and covered her face with her hands. She took a deep breath before looking up. Ivar feared he would see tears, so he was unprepared for the fury she turned on him.

"How could you, even for a minute, think I would want that? When I have fought to save your life, you think I would want you to die just to be with me?" Lena shook her head again. "Perhaps you can appease your father with a trial marriage. If the two of you are suited, then a true marriage can move forward. If you don't suit, then neither of you will be bound to the other. Eindride will take me to Kaupang."

"No!" Ivar bellowed. "Absolutely not. You are not running away with my best friend. I will kill him if he's touched you."

Ivar reared back and stood from the bed. Lena watched the man who had just made love to her turn into a berserker. Her own temper flared as indignation consumed her.

"Touched me? You think I'm whoring myself to your best friend? He has never touched me. No man but you has, and you know it! How could you accuse me, or Eindride for that matter, of being so disloyal?"

"You just admitted you're going to run away with him," Ivar snarled.

"Run away with him? No, I said he would take me to Kaupang. Ein isn't going to stay. He wants me about as much as I want him, which is not at all. Ein has his sights set on Brenna, and she welcomes his attention."

"Lena, I never said you are a whore. I can't stand that word being said about you."

"Then all the more reason for me to leave, because your bride believes I am one. She said as much."

"What?" Ivar exploded all over again.

"Nothing. I'm going to Kaupang. I have an uncle and an aunt who would take me in. I can find work there or sell my sword arm to a neighboring jarl."

"Stop. Stop jumping from one subject to another hoping to confuse and distract me. You are not going to Kaupang or anywhere else. Your home is here. You are not traveling anywhere with Eindride unless he plans to die an early death. You are not traveling with anyone but me. And just what did Inga say to you?"

Ivar stood with his arms crossed, and Lena's eyes

gravitated to the rippling muscles across his chest and forearms. She closed her eyes before shifting her gaze to Ivar's eyes. His heated stare was thunderous, and she forgot what they were arguing about as desire pooled in her core. Her breathing hitched, and Ivar's nostrils flared when her desire registered. He stalked around the bed and used his size to inch Lena back against the wall. His forearms bracketed her head as her heart pounded.

"Tell me what she said," Ivar whispered in her ear before flicking her lobe with his tongue then sucking it into his mouth. "Tell me what she said, and I will ease the ache between your legs."

Ivar pressed his hardened rod against her belly, then tilted his hips to rub against her mons.

Lena licked her dry lips as her fingers itched to reach out for him. Her eyes drifted shut as two of Ivar's questing fingers sought her entrance. She gasped as he thrust them into her.

"Tell me, and I will fill you with my cock. That's what you want, what you need isn't it?"

Lena wrapped her hand around Ivar's cock and began stroking.

"You know it's what I want. But I also know it's what you want, too. I don't want to talk about that woman right now. If you want me to ride you, then you leave this topic alone."

Ivar thrust into her hand as his fingers continued to work Lena's heated flesh. Their plan to seduce each other into submission was working too well. Their lips fused together as they battled each other, their tongues dueling. Ivar's sudden withdrawal from her sheath, made Lena cry out in pain, the flaming ache within her core overwhelming her. She stroked faster as her deep blue eyes flashed shards of ice at Ivar. He might withhold pleasure from her, but she would overwhelm him with it. She used her free hand to lift her breast in offering to Ivar, massaging the flesh, then tweaking the nipple before offering it to him again. His head fell to her breast as he sank to his knees, tearing himself from her hand. He suckled hard before biting her nipple just enough to elicit a deep moan. He hooked one of her legs over his shoulder before returning to his earlier feast.

"Tell me," he growled.

Lena waited for the sensation of his tongue against her nether lips before sighing and relenting.

"She said she was your wife."

"I already heard that." Ivar paused his ministrations long enough to respond.

"She called me a whore. And maybe I am, but I don't care because right now, your head is between my thighs and not hers."

Ivar rose to his feet and grabbed Lena's hand. He led her to the bed and turned her to face it.

"Up," he commanded, and Lena's eagerness to obey excited him.

Ivar ran his fingers over the round globes presented before him as Lena tilted forward to rest on her forearms. He palmed one then the other before bringing his hand down in a heavy slap. Lena's moan drove him to spank her once more before trailing a finger along the crevice between her bottom. He tapped his finger against her sacred hole before carrying on to her slick entrance.

"Do you think I will ever give either of these up? You hold claim to my cock just as I hold claim to these. I'm going to fuck you now, Lena. I want to hear you scream my name as I pound into you."

"Ivar, now. Don't make me wait."

"But waiting is part of the fun."

"No, it's not." Lena shook her head. "Are you trying to be cruel?"

"You've always played along in the past. You've found the wait exciting."

"This is different, and you know it."

"Different?" Ivar thrust into her, and her moan filled the chamber. "Different because you want me to claim you? To show you I want no other? Because you need me inside you? Need me to prove I don't want anyone else?"

"Yes," Lena sobbed as Ivar's thrusts shook the bed. "Because I need it before we must say our goodbyes."

Ivar's hand came down in a bruising spank.

"If you speak of us separating once more, I shall spank you in earnest. Lena, no more."

Rather than argue, Lena forced her body to relax and let the sensations of their bodies coming together consume her. Ivar sensed when she relented, and he became man possessed, driven to surge into her over and over until he saw stars before his eyes. His own groans and pants muffled Lena's moans.

"Ivar!" Lena screamed as her climax swept through every cell and hair of her body.

"Lena!" Ivar's bellow matched hers as his seed jetted from him, leaving him wholly drained.

They collapsed on the bed, Ivar's body wrapped around Lena's as her back pressed against his chest. They drifted off without a word.

FIVE

Ivar awoke with a stretch then reached for Lena, but his hand only touched a tepid spot where she had lain beside him while they slept. He paused when he heard voices in the main chamber of the longhouse. He was aware Lena's father, Tormud, was home from the fields. Ivar looked to the window and realized it was already past the evening meal. His father would be livid that he did not attend. Soren would have expected him to lavish attention on Inga and pretend to be a doting groom. He was anything but that, unless his bride would be Lena. Ivar searched for his clothes in the dim light but decided against putting them back on. He and Lena had awoken once earlier, and while Lena watched, Ivar used an ewer of water and a bar of soap to bathe. It had been freezing, but at least he had washed the top layer of grime from him. Now, he looked to the pegs on the wall and spotted the spare clothes he kept at Lena's home. He hurried to dress before stepping into the main room. Lena glanced over from where she sat beside the fire with a spindle as she worked wool into yarn. She smiled at him before turning back to her grandmother. Ivar made his way to the large table in the center of the main chamber. They set a place for him beside Tormud, and his growling stomach testified to his hunger.

"Join me. You've been away a long time. A hot meal would do you some good. You've looking thin." Tormud thumbed the table beside with his meaty fist. He had been a warrior in his younger days, but a deep slash in his leg left him with a limp. He had become a farmer to remain close to his family. Lena's younger brother, Jan, stumbled through the door with three buckets hanging from his arms. At sixteen, Jan was still all arms and legs, but within a year, he would raid with the rest of them. Ivar lifted two buckets, and Jan pushed the door closed behind him.

"Lena," her younger brother beamed at her as they embraced. "I'm glad you're home. That damned cow doesn't like me."

Jan pulled up a pant leg to show a nasty bruise that was still bright blue and yellow. Lena shook her head but laughed.

"I told you she doesn't like cold hands," Lena's laughter turned to giggles, and Ivar was certain his heart would explode. Contentedness filled Lena when she was with her family, and they enjoyed one another's company. It was so unlike his own home where his father and mother barely looked at one another, and his mother blamed his father for Ivar's brothers' deaths. The tension was almost palpable in his home. It was why he spent most nights here.

"Maybe. Anyway, here's the water you asked for." Jan turned towards Ivar and grinned. "My sister insisted you would need a bath. I think she just wants an excuse to--"

Lena cut Jan off with a sharp elbow jammed into his side. Ivar looked over to see Lena's cheeks were a bright shade of red. There was a silent agreement that no one discussed his physical relationship with Lena in front of her father. Her father graciously turned a blind eye when they retired together. Ivar took his seat where Tormud had indicated, the spot he usually occupied, and picked up the heel of bread near his trencher. He spooned *skouse*, a thick stew, into his trencher before dipping a hunk of bread into it. He realized not enough time had passed for Lena to have made the stew, so he turned towards Amma.

"Thank for you the supper. It's just what I needed to put some meat back on my bones, Amma. You spoil us."

"It is the privilege of age. I can do whatever I want, and spoiling the men of my family is what I want."

Ivar cast a glance at Lena and saw the strain around her eyes and mouth when Amma spoke of him as family. He bit into another chunk of bread, but before he swallowed, the door to the longhouse swung open, and his father stood in the doorway.

"I was certain I would find you here. You look well rested, son. Like a man who's had his cock pleased and now his stomach."

Ivar pushed back on the bench so hard that even Tormud had to grasp the table. He lurched across the room when two of his father's guards moved towards Lena. He reached her in time to push her behind him and pulled a knife from his belt.

"What are you doing here, Father? Besides insulting my companion and her family."

"Your *companion*," Soren sneered, "assaulted a jarl's daughter this afternoon. I will arrest and hold her until I am ready to dole out her punishment."

"She did no such thing," Ivar boomed, but before he said more, Lena tugged on his sleeve and stepped around him.

"I did not assault Inga. She grabbed my hair and held me underwater while I bathed. I did nothing more than defend myself."

"What?" Ivar hissed. His father infuriated him, and Lena frustrated him. That was the key portion of the story she avoided telling him earlier. He hoped his expression told her she should have told him before he discovered it this way.

"Did she not tell you? I suppose you were both too busy. Your concubine threw your bride into a tub in front of several witnesses."

"Jarl Soren, I heard about that," Jan stepped forward. "Inga insulted my sister, but Lena didn't respond. So instead of leaving her alone, Inga tried to drown her. All the women were talking about how easy Lena let Inga off."

Soren's glare shifted towards Jan, but he stood tall beside Ivar, placing Lena her devoted lover and her devoted brother. While Jan was still lanky, he had the height and broad shoulders of his father, which made him taller than the jarl.

"No one was talking to you, whelp."

"Perhaps not, but there were plenty of people talking in the village today. It seems Inga got what she deserved. She's been rude to many women, even the frú herself, while she has been here." Jan took a deep breath that broadened his chest considerably more than anyone realized he could. He transformed from Lena's little brother to her fiercest protector and a battle-ready warrior. "I am surprised you hadn't heard of it by now. People have been grumbling since the day she arrived. She is an unwanted guest. Like vermin in a bed."

"You shall lose that loose tongue of yours, boy." Soren stepped towards Jan, who took his own step forward. Lena watched with eyes as wide as saucers as she clutched Ivar's sleeve and kept pulling. Neither of them could do anything to protect Jan, who had sworn his oath of fealty to Soren years ago. He had decided to stand up to Soren as a man, and he would have to meet the consequences as a man. However, Tormud did not seem to see it the same way. He limped between Soren and Jan.

"Jarl, my son speaks the truth," he turned his head towards his son, "even when he shouldn't. Honesty is a dangerous trait at times. So is blind trust."

"And who is it that you think is in danger, other than your foolish son?"

"As I said, honesty is a dangerous trait. I have two children and a mother to care for. I have nothing more to say." Tormud pushed Jan towards the table and out of Soren's reach before turning to stand before Lena. "But if I were to say more, it would be to note that the people of this village have already chosen the right one, and they don't place their trust in one who will disappoint and betray them."

"What are you blabbering about?" Soren curled his lip in disgust.

"He means, Father, that no one in this homestead wants Inga as their next frú. They don't trust her, and you shouldn't either. You want the alliance, but you aren't willing to see that it will weaken us instead. The clan knows Lena is the best choice to help lead the next generation. You refuse to see what is clearly there for the sake of an alliance we already have."

"An alliance that isn't forged in blood, bonded bloodlines. Your concubine is nothing."

Ivar lunged at his father but did not touch him.

"Do not call her that." Ivar's hushed tones were too quiet for anyone but his father to hear the menace. "She is my companion, and she will be my wife. If you make me choose between her and my fealty to you, you will find yourself without an heir."

"You don't threaten me," his father's voice carried the same warning.

"I don't threaten weaker men. I only make promises." Ivar stepped back and stood to his full height, and for the first time in his life, he saw a flash of fear in his father's eyes.

"Keep her out of sight until Thor and his family depart."

"With Inga."

"Yes. With her. She will return in two months for the wedding."

Soren and his guards departed, and Ivar pulled Lena into his arms.

"That's two months to plan," Ivar brushed a kiss against her temple as she wrapped her arms around him and relaxed as he enfolded her in his embrace.

"Yes. Two months to plan." She suspected her plans would not be the same as Ivar's, but she lacked the strength to argue again.

SIX

Lena sheathed her weapon and wiped the sweat from her brow as she smiled at the woman with whom she had been sparring. The fight exhausted her, but she was satisfied with the day's training. She had worked harder during the past three weeks than she had since she was first made a shieldmaiden. Their visitors had departed the morning after the confrontation in her home, and she had kept herself as busy as she could during the day. She refused to give Jarl Soren any reason to speak poorly of her. She had suggested to Ivar that he spend his nights in his home under his parents' roof, but he had exploded and refused. While they still craved one another, a distance had developed between them when they were not making love. She glanced towards where Ivar and Vigo continued their mock battle. Ivar had stripped off his tunic, and his skin glistened with sweat in the warm autumn sun. She wanted to run her hands over every muscle as they twitch and bunch as she caressed him. She had the same visceral reaction whenever she saw his chiseled form. Weeks earlier, she would have indulged herself and called him away from sparring with Vigo, so they could run back to her home or into the surrounding trees. Now she avoided being seen with Ivar in public, fearing his father's wrath.

Lena looked toward the jarl's longhouse, where thralls would serve the evening meal soon. The long hours of daylight made time deceptive. Her belly rumbled, so it had to be early evening. Pounding hoofbeats and a woman's voice pulled Lena's attention away. She looked towards the gate as the most beautiful woman she had ever seen rode through. The woman's flaxen hair had come loose from her braid, but she rode as though she had been born on horseback. When the woman reined in, Lena saw the rider was close to falling off her horse in exhaustion. Lena ran to her as the beautiful stranger listed to one side.

"Ivar!" Lena called as she grabbed the horse's bridle to keep it steady. She heard Ivar approach and looked over in time to see Ivar catch the woman as she fell from her saddle.

"Who is she?" Ivar looked around, peering through the gate expecting to see either guards or pursuers, but the woman was alone.

Lena stepped next to Ivar and Eindride, who had run over when Vigo turned to practice with another warrior. Lena's brow crinkled as she looked at the young woman who was about her age. There was something about the woman that seemed foreign despite being dressed like any other Norse woman. Her coloring was also different despite the blonde hair.

"She's Scots," Lena murmured. Robin's-egg blue eyes fluttered open, and a scowl formed on the otherwise angelic face.

"Highlander, lass. Nae Scots. Highlander." There was a bite to the words even if the voice was breathy and tired.

"Whatever you may be or wherever you're from, you need food and rest."

"Aye. I canna disagree with that." The stranger looked from Lena to Ivar and seemed to shrink. "Put me down. Please."

"Ivar, carry her to my home, then put her down."

"Nay. I can walk. The earth stopped spinning once ma horse stopped galloping. I'm well enough now."

Ivar looked at Lena, unsure of what to do until Lena nodded. He eased the petite woman to her feet and then let Lena step in.

"What's your name?" Lena asked softly.

"Lorna Mackay."

"Mackay? As in Rangvald's woman?" Ivar blurted.

Lena stifled a laugh as the Highland lass turned into a Highland warrior, hand on her sword.

"I am nae that wretched mon's woman. He can burn in the deepest fires of hell for all I care."

"*Hel* doesn't have fire. She is the goddess of only one realm after death."

"Nae yer *hel*. Ma hell. The Christian one that has fire and a devil to chase Rang around for eternity. May he burn there."

"Ivar, you know who Lorna is?" Eindride cast an appreciative gaze over her, only to receive a snarl in return.

"Rangvald mentioned her one night. Seems Rangvald rescued Lorna during a raid on her clan and brought her back to the Trondelag. He's been obsessed with her since," Ivar spoke the last sentence as a whisper, but he was not quiet enough, because Lorna spat next to his boot.

"Obsessed? He would have had to pay attention to me to be obsessed. The louse brought me to a foreign land claiming I would have a better life here but abandons me to his witch of a mother. Then, when he finally remembers I exist, he makes false promises when he's already promised to another."

"Rangvald's not promised to anyone," Ivar's brow furrowed.

"He may nae have been three weeks ago, but he is now." Lorna huffed and crossed her arms.

"Will you come to my home, please? I can offer you a hot bath and something to eat. We're close in size, so I have fresh clothes you can wear." Lena reached out her hand to Lorna, and after only a moment's hesitation, their foreign guest stepped forward. Lena shot Ivar a quelling glance as she turned toward her home.

The two women walked in silence until they reached Lena's home. She opened the door and ushered Lorna in. Her grandmother was visiting her aunt and uncle as they grieved together. The longhouse was empty, so she pulled dried beef, a wheel of cheese, a heel of bread, and assorted dried fruit from the larder. She placed them on the table with a knife next to the cheese. She left the knife for Lorna as a test, but when the woman began to shovel dried beef and fruit into her mouth as though she had not eaten in a month of Sundays, Lena went about heating water for a bath. By the time the bath was ready, Lorna had devoured everything in sight.

"I ken. I have an unusually healthy appetite for a lass ma size. Ma da and brothers were relentless in their teasing me aboot it."

"You haven't eaten any more than I would have after riding for four days. You're welcome to anything you need while you are here. If you grow hungry again, you but have to ask, and I will be sure you have what you want."

Lorna swept her gaze over Lena as she stripped off her travel-stained clothes. There were many things about them that were similar enough that they might have passed for sisters if neither spoke.

"Thank ye," Lorna smiled. "Ye're a shieldmaiden, aye? I can tell from how ye move and stand."

"I am. I would venture to say you are a warrior, too. But I didn't think the Scots let their women fight."

"They dinna. But Highlanders do. At least when there is an absolute need. They dinna take to the notion as ye Norse do. Ma da, God rest his soul, didna see any harm in me learning to wield a sword, and with three aulder brothers, God rest their souls too, it was a way to keep me amused and oot from under ma mother's feet. Ma brothers didna mind when we were younger, then it became a game to see which of their friends I could best. All the while, I improved and got stronger. They even took me raiding cattle a few times."

"You must be more at home than you expected. Rangvald's people have shieldmaidens too. There were women for you to train with." Lena snapped her mouth shut when she realized that she assumed Lorna was a free woman. Lorna did not wear a torc around her neck or a fealty ring around her wrist, but that did not mean she had not pulled them off during her flight from Rangvald's homestead.

"I'm not a thrall. I never was. Rang brought me as a free woman."

"Rang?" Lena picked up on the familiarity Lorna used when mentioning a man well above her station.

"We are of equal standing." Lorna tilted her chin up and dared Lena to disagree. "Ma da was the laird of ma clan, and I was his only daughter. Rangvald offered me a home after his brother killed ma parents and left with me nothing. I am a free woman, even if

I work within another woman's home. I get to train, and it is all I had to look forward to."

"But Ivar made it sound as though you and Rangvald were more involved than just--" Lena trailed off and shrugged.

"I'm nothing to Rangvald but an inconvenience. Someone he regrets bringing back with him." The bitterness and pain in Lorna's voice echoed in Lena's ears. She would become the same thing to Ivar once he married Inga. The two women remained silent as Lorna bathed and put on a long tunic that fit her as well as it did Lena. With few words exchanged, Lena led Lorna to the jarl's longhouse, knowing they would have to present the unexpected guest before the jarl and frú sooner rather than later.

"Come stay with me," Ivar whispered in Lena's ear as they ate the evening meal together. Lorna sat across from them with Brenna, the woman Eindride was courting, sitting beside him. Lena cast her gaze sideways and shook her head.

"You heard my father. He expects Lorna to stay here since she is a noble guest. She may be only a free woman here, but my father is enamored with being able to say he has a Scottish noblewoman under his roof. I don't trust him not to seduce her at best, accost her at worst."

"Your mother would never allow that," Lena whispered from the side of her mouth.

"She's never been able to stop him before. Lena, please. I'm asking for Rangvald's sake. The man is in love with her. Anyone who was nearby realized it when he and I spoke of marriage. And I'm asking you for her sake. I fear what my father might do."

"You think I can stop him? He's more likely to have me fastened to the *niðstöng*. I have no desire for your father to shackle me to the shame-pole where the entire village can throw things are me in scorn."

"He won't do that."

"Are you really that naïve?" Lena turned her head to look at Ivar for the first time since they began whispering.

"He won't harm you because he knows I will retaliate."

"Ivar, listen to yourself. You're willing to fight your father, kill him even, because of me. That is not what I want, and it won't make our lives any happier if you do. It'll only get your killed, too."

"That wasn't what I meant. I may hate the man, but I won't commit patricide. He knows I will sabotage other alliances instead."

Lena took a deep breath. They would only go around in circles if she continued to argue with him. She nodded, and Ivar squeezed her hand under the table.

Over the next fortnight, Lena moved into the jarl's house much to Soren's anger and dismay. She kept herself out of sight except at meals. Living in the jarl's home made it easier for her to complete her daily routine. In the mornings, Ivar greeted her and Lorna before walking to the main hall to break their fast together. Both women set to work in the kitchen before spending the afternoon training. Lorna had only asked for a place to stay and work. She was willing to fight—since she came with her sword and shield—in exchange for a bed at night. She and Lorna shared a chamber, and every night their barred their door against unwanted nighttime visitors. The first two nights, someone tried to enter the chamber, but was unsuccessful. Lena shook her head and held her finger against her lips the first night. It was not Ivar, because he would have announced himself. The second night, the two women sat ready with knives in their hands. The door rattled and muffled curses drifted beneath the door, but nothing more.

Lena and Lorna walked off the training field together. They had pushed one another until they were both drenched in sweat but laughing about how they had each taken turns sliding in the mud. They had offered one another a hand to stand more than once. They had been training all afternoon, and both women needed baths and fresh clothes before they would be presentable for the evening meal.

"I'm headed to bathe before the evening meal. I canna stomach the smell of that dung I stepped in earlier." Lorna grinned at Lena as she waved before heading to the longhouse for fresh clothes.

Ivar stepped behind Lena and nuzzled the skin beneath her ear.

"I've missed you," he murmured as he kissed her neck.

"Mmm. I can tell." Lena pressed her backside against Ivar's obvious arousal. "Let's slip back to my home and bathe together there. My father and Jan will still be in the fields. Amma won't say anything."

"That sounds perfect. I'm always happy to assist you with your bath, my love."

Neither said more before guardsmen announced approaching riders. Ivar and Lena walked towards the gates, stunned to see Rangvald ride through with a contingent of guards with him. He looked in much the same state as Lorna had when she arrived, except the stench of alcohol wafted off of him before Ivar and Lena reached his side.

"Rangvald?" Ivar grasped the man's shoulders before he fell backwards after dismounting, or rather slithering, from his horse. "What brings you here?"

"My seester, of course. You haven't married her

yeeet." Rangvald's slurred speech was only further proof that he was drunk.

"I know I haven't. Things have not been going so smoothly with the negotiations."

"I know. It's because of her," Rangvald lifted a weak finger to point in Lena's direction. When Ivar leaned in to grab Rangvald's tunic, the other man tapped Ivar on the chest. "Lucky man that you are. At least the woman you love wants you. Miiine caaan't stand me."

"Do you mean Lorna?" Lena asked quietly.

Rangvald's head jerked up from where it seemed to dangle from his neck.

"You know her? How?" Rangvald demanded. He looked around as though he only now realized where he stood. "Is she here? Is this where she ran to?"

Rangvald tried to push Ivar out of his way, but Ivar grabbed hold.

"You need to sober up, my friend, and you need to bathe."

"What I neeed is my woooman." Rangvald stuttered. "And another drink."

Lena snatched the wineskin from Rangvald's hand and shook her head.

"She won't want to see you to begin with, and she definitely won't be willing to talk to you in this state. Ivar, get him sober while I delay Lorna."

Lena spun on her heels and dashed toward the bathhouse. She had no idea how to keep Lorna occupied until Ivar got Rangvald sober enough to not humiliate himself or ruin his chance with Lorna.

By the time the evening meal started, Lena was on edge. She tried to quiet the jealousy that had taken root since Rangvald arrived, but she could not stop envying Lorna since it was obvious Rangvald would go to extremes to have her. While Rangvald and Signy had traveled with their father for the last negotiations, Rangvald's older brother Harold and his younger brother Sven had stayed home to oversee their homestead. As a second son, Rangvald would be free to marry who he wanted, and it was clear he wanted Lorna. Ivar did not have such a luxury. Things had been tenuous between the two tribes, and now the hold up in negotiations was causing more tension as reports of border raids came every day. Soren's herders stole from Thor's only to have Thor's shepherd steal back their flocks and take some extra. They went back and forth.

Lena guided Lorna into the gathering hall and tried to keep her new best friend occupied as she searched for Ivar and Rangvald. Lorna gasped, and Lena was certain Lorna had spotted Rangvald. Lorna covered her mouth, but her eyes widened with shock as Rangvald leaped over the table and crashed through the crowd to reach Lorna. In turn, she spun and dashed out of the longhouse. Lena turned to follow them, but Ivar caught her around the waist.

"Leave them. They need to sort this out for themselves."

"I know. I'm just worried she'll kill him first." Lena was not joking. Try as she might, she had not gotten the finer details of what transpired between Lorna and Rangvald, and she had not learned why Lorna had run other than because Lorna thought Rangvald had broken a promise. She feared Lorna might gut him like a fattened pig. Lorna was as fine a warrior as any shieldmaiden if not better. She pushed Lena to her limits every time they sparred, but the woman never seemed to break a sweat nor have a hair out of place. If she had not frightened all the other men, she would have had a line of admirers.

. . .

Ivar and Lena watched in alternating horror and amusement as Rangvald spent the next week pining for Lorna and trying to convince her to return home. The man lost weight and seemed a shell of himself except for the moments when he saw Lorna. She tried to avoid him, but he arranged for her to train with any weapon of her choice rather than just her sword. He ensured thralls sent trays of food to her chamber when she refused to join them for evening meals, and he managed to have clothes delivered to Lorna's chamber when she refused Lena's offer of more gowns rather than leather pants and tunics. Lena moved into Ivar's chamber when each night Rangvald took up guard outside the chamber she had shared with Lorna.

It took only a week for Lorna to see how her rejection affected Rangvald. He was a man in love and in pain. Their reconciliation brought sighs to everyone as the drama played out between a couple who were fated for one another. They left with Lorna riding in front of Rangvald as he wrapped his arms around her waist.

The only disappointment for Ivar and Lena was that they finalized the betrothal, and Inga would arrive for a trial marriage within a fortnight. The weight of the world was crushing Lena as Inga's arrival drew nearer. She waffled between wanting to cling to Ivar during every possible moment and putting distance between them so they would be virtual strangers by the time Inga arrived. Ivar left her with little choice since he refused to be more than an arm's reach from her.

SEVEN

"He will have my head, Lena. No. Absolutely not. No." Eindride shook his head as he continued to saddle his horse.

"Then I will go on my own." Lena stepped beside Eindride and waited for her friend to look at her. "I don't want to go to Kaupang any more than you want to take me, but I have to go. Ivar will not go through with the marriage if I am still here."

"And we will all breathe easier for that."

"Until things with Thor's tribe fall so far apart that nothing short of a war will fix it. We need this alliance, even if no one wants it. Thor's numbers and strength are greater than ours. We would not stand a chance if he waged a full attack." Lena stroked the flank of Eindride's horse as she pleaded with him. "I don't dare travel that far alone. Even I'm not the impulsive. But I can't stay here. This isn't about what either Ivar or I want. It's about what's right for our people."

"You'd give up that easily?" Eindride looked down at the woman his best friend loved with a passion he hoped he one day possessed for the woman he chose.

"It's not about giving up," Lena bellowed before

taking a calming voice. "I'm sick of people saying that. Damn it, I don't want to give Ivar up. I don't want to watch him with another woman, see his child grow in another woman's belly, but I also won't make him sacrifice his life for me. If he weren't his father's only heir, Soren would have killed him already for disobeying him. I fear for Ivar's life. Sometimes Soren's gaze is so dark and menacing that I'm terrified he will harm Ivar regardless of not having another heir."

"What you say is true. I've seen those looks, too. But you understand just as well as I do that Ivar won't stay here to greet Inga. He will chase after you. Then what? He won't stop until he has you on his horse and then in his bed. What will that get any of us? Soren is likely to kill you for interfering with the wedding. And me along with you. That's not the welcome home I want."

"So, you expect me to stay? To watch another woman with the only man I've ever loved? The only man who has ever touched me."

"Lena, if there was another way, I would help you. You must realize I would. It's been the three of us since we were children, but I've sworn fealty to Soren, and I won't let either you or Ivar throw away your lives."

"You'd just have us live in misery." Lena shook her head and stepped around Eindride. She turned the corner while looking back at Eindride in disgust, so she was unprepared for the wall of muscle she walked into. She squeaked as strong hands gripped her shoulders. Her head whipped around, and her blue eyes met hazel eyes filled with fury.

Ivar could not believe what he had heard. Lena still wanted to run away to Kaupang, and she was still trying to enlist Eindride's help. He bent low enough to scoop Lena over his shoulder. His large hand landed a swat to her backside, and she yelped more from surprise than pain. Ivar marched across the homestead, uncaring of the scene they made. He swung the door to Lena's home open and was thankful that no one was inside. He dropped Lena to her feet and only barely caught her hand in time to keep her from falling. Ivar locked and barred the door before turning towards her. Lena put both hands up and shook her head as she tried to inch away.

"Don't shake your head at me, woman. You intended to coerce our friend into helping you run away. You claim it's because it's the right thing to do, but I think you're too coward to fight for us. I think you mean more to me than I do to you. I'm the only one trying to keep us together. If you don't want me, then say as much, Lena. Otherwise, I will fight to my dying breath to keep us together."

"How dare you call me a coward? Do you have any idea how the thought of seeing you with another woman tears me apart? But do you see me falling apart? No, because I have no choice in this. Fate is not in my hands. It's not even in your hands. Have you thought about what it will be like when you see me with a husband? When I carry another man's child? Is that something you look forward to?"

Ivar lunged and pulled Lena against him, his fingers biting into her upper arms. He shook her before claiming her mouth in a punishing and possessive kiss.

"The only fucking husband you will ever have is me. And no woman will carry my child but you, since I will not be sticking my cock in anyone but you. I will kill any man who thinks he can have you. Can have what is mine."

Lena shook her head as her eyes welled with tears. She buried her head against his chest and thumped her fist against his chest, but it was more in capitulation than defense.

"Why are you doing this to me?" she sobbed. "You know you're going to marry her. You're taunting me with a future I can't have. And when you marry her, are you damning me to a life alone? You know I won't be any man's mistress. Not even yours. I won't lead you to dishonor a wife and your people. Will you scare away any man who thinks to court me? Why can you marry but I can't? I don't want to grow old alone with memories that can't even keep me warm."

"So you'd rather marry a man you don't love?"

"You might grow to love Inga, just as I might grow to love another man."

"Ha," Ivar's laugh was more of a bark. "I could never love that woman. But you want to find another man to love. Do you already have someone in mind? Eindride perhaps? After all it would take you more than a week to travel alone together to Kaupang."

"Don't! Don't do that. Don't bring our friend into this when he's innocent. You know as well as I do that he's in love with Brenna, even if he hasn't figured it out yet. I would never take a man from another woman. There's no one else. No one but you. But there could be."

Ivar cupped her cheeks and tipped her head back. His thumbs brushed away the tears as his own slid down his cheeks.

"I'm not giving you up. You won't need to find another man. You have the only one you need right before you. I will work this out. I will make things right but don't leave. Eindride is right. I would only come after you. Lena, I need you. I need your strength and your wisdom to navigate the next few weeks. My father will push me to my limits, and I need you by my side. I trust you, and I rely on your opinion. I have no idea how soon I can make it happen, but Inga will return home, and it will be for good."

Lena nodded. In that moment, she resolved herself to accept whatever fate had in store for them. She would not fight it. The gods planned their destiny, and it wasn't theirs to change. Ivar would succeed in ending the marriage contract, or he would not. She would have patience as things played out. If Ivar married Inga, she would sort out her future then. She would find someone to marry and begin a new life with a husband, or she would leave and start over somewhere else. But fighting Ivar was not doing either of them any good. She preferred to enjoy the time they had.

"I believe there was spanking you think I deserve." Lena leaned back and offered him an impish grin. Ivar's smile was predatory as he followed her into her chamber, kicking the door shut as he pounced. He knocked them both to the bed where they landed, tangled arms and legs while locked in a passionate kiss. They passed the rest of the afternoon making love until they were both too exhausted to remain awake. No one disturbed them until morning.

EIGHT

"Ivar!" Banging at Lena's chamber door woke them both. "Ivar! Get up. Inga and her family are only a mile away. The guards have already spotted them. Wake up!"

Eindride pounded his fist against the door until Ivar ripped it open, standing naked before his friend. "I heard you. And I am awake, but not the way I want to be. I will be there." Ivar went to shut the door, but Eindride's foot shot forward, and Eindride pushed the door back open.

"I'm sorry, but I don't trust you not to fall back into bed then lose track of time." Eindride nodded in Lena's direction but refused to look at her as she sat with the sheet tucked under her arms. "Lena's too much of a distraction. You have to come now. Your father won't punish you for this. He'll punish Lena and her family. Hurry, please."

Eindride retreated and let the door close. Ivar looked at Lena, her blonde hair wild from their night of passion. He sat on the edge of the bed beside her and held her chin between his thumb and forefinger. He kissed her before nibbling on her lower lip.

"How I want to stay here and do that all day," he sighed before claiming another languid kiss. He leaned forward, pressing Lena into the mattress. He yanked the sheet out of the way and climbed over her, coming to rest his weight on his forearms. "I'm going to make love to you again, my darling."

"No, you're not," came a booming voice from the other side of the door. "Ivar, I'm serious. I'll drag you out of there if it's the only way to save Lena."

Ivar's head dropped as he shook it. "He's right," he whispered.

"I know." Lena kissed his forehead before pushing him away.

They hurried through their morning ablutions and dressed quickly. The three friends had only stepped into the open clearing in the middle of the homestead when horses galloped through the gate. Ivar swept his gaze over the visitors, looking for Rangvald. He did not spare a glance for Inga, and he heard a gasp from one rider. His gazed shifted, and he saw blazing hatred coming from his betrothed's eyes. She had perceived Ivar's disinterest as a slight, and he did not feel guilty. He smiled, but the warmth never made it to his eyes. He looked once more for Rangvald and found him mounted with Lorna seated before him. Lena was already moving towards them, but she halted when Inga's voice filled the air with her whining tone.

"What is that whore still doing here? Father, you promised me Jarl Soren had dealt with her. Why was she walking out of a house with my husband this morning? She walked out with two men? Is that the man my husband is? He likes to share? He won't be sharing me."

"If you don't shut up, Inga, you won't have a husband to worry about," Rangvald growled as he dismounted, then helped Lorna to the ground. Rangvald and Lorna stepped forward, and Ivar and Lena greeted them.

"She's a right wee beastie, that one," Lorna whispered.

"I heard that!" Inga bellowed as she turned in her saddle to see her brother and the others. "You're no better than her. Worse even, since you're a savage and a whore."

Rangvald was beside his sister's horse in a heartbeat, lifting her from the saddle. He leaned close enough that no one heard, but Inga's face blanched, and she nodded when Rangvald straightened. She did not utter another world.

Soren and Disa stepped forward to greet their guests. Disa was still a stunning woman despite a hard life with an angry and spiteful husband. She had lost three of her four children, but she continued to serve her people despite her everlasting grief. Disa moved to greet her guests. She ushered Inga, her mother, and Signy toward the jarl's longhouse, but before she walked away, she turned back and waved for Lorna to join them. Disa turned a sad smile toward Lena as she waited for Lorna.

Torn between her friend and being accepted by a noblewoman, Lorna was not sure where to go. She looked back at Rangvald, but he was talking to Ivar and his brothers Harold and Sven. The entire family had traveled for the wedding. Lena nudged Lorna toward the longhouse.

"Go. You are to be part of their family. Claim your position now. Disa will take care of you, and she will make you welcome. I'm certain Signy will appreciate having you there. She is so different from the spitefulness of her sister and mother Ulfhild."

"She is. It's hard to believe she's related to them. It must be her gift."

Lena nodded. She had thought more than once that she might ask Signy what she saw of her own future, but she feared what the young woman might tell her. Lorna followed the other women, and Lena remained only to find the men had moved away to tend to the horses. They left her standing in the middle of the green by herself. It seemed to signify her life at that moment.

"I don't envy you one bit," Rangvald laughed as Ivar glared at him. "She's my sister, but she can't leave soon enough. She's wretched to Lorna and Signy."

"And you think she'll be better here?" Ivar looked over his shoulder to see the group of women walking into his family's longhouse. He also noticed Lena standing alone, looking tiny against the village backdrop. He wanted to go to her, whisk her away, and take her to a place where they created their own happy family. Ivar watched as she glanced around and then, shoulders hunched against a cool breeze, walked back to her own longhouse.

"I wish there were another way to seal this alliance, rid us of my sister, and spare you a disastrous marriage like our own parents have." Rangvald shook his head as he continued to curry his horse.

"I've been trying to think of a solution, too, but even if I didn't marry Inga, my father still wouldn't consent to Lena. He'd just find me another jarl's daughter to marry."

"She's still very young at only sixteen. Perhaps, away from our mother, she will mature into a warmer, more caring woman." Sven spoke up for the first time. He was the youngest of Rangvald's siblings, but favored Rangvald and Signy's temperament more than Harold's and Inga's. Sven did not look convinced, though, when he finished with "One can hope."

"My mother might be a good influence on her as

far as being a frú to my people, but the animosity between my parents won't teach Inga any lessons on how to be a good wife." Ivar's stomach twisted and bile rose in his throat as he thought of Inga as his wife. He barely stood the thought of being in the same room as her, fully dressed at that. He did not want to picture having to bed her. He imagined she would issue commands throughout the entire coupling while lying like a dead herring, not even twitching.

"Take a firm hand with her," grunted Harold. Ivar nodded but did not dare to look in the other man's direction. No one missed the irony of his comment. He had lost one of his hands during a raid in Scotland, when he attacked Lorna and her mother and Lorna defended herself. Ivar wondered how that family dynamic was working out. He glanced at Rangvald, but his friend gave a quick shake of his head.

"My sister needs a man who will teach her some sense, and a firm hand is the only way to do it. Our father has spoiled her," Harold continued. "While Father may fear few things, he shies away from Signy. He worries she will tell him his fate, and it won't be one he likes. Instead, he dotes on Inga. She has our mother's tongue and can do no wrong in Father's eyes."

"If I didn't know better, I would think all three of you are warning me away from your sister. What would happen to the alliance?"

"Father hasn't thought to ask any of us how we feel about your tribe. He assumes we carry the same dislike and distrust that he always has." Harold glanced over his shoulder before lowering his voice. "Neither my brothers nor I care to keep the dispute going. We see no sense in losing more warriors and cattle. We would rather come to an agreement where we are all satisfied, and no one is shackled to our sister."

"Would you swear to an alliance once you are jarl? Even if I didn't marry Inga?" Ivar was unconvinced by Harold's suggestion. If it had come from Rangvald, he would have believed it, but he trusted Harold as little as he did his father, Thor. Unfortunately, Harold was Thor's heir, not Rangvald.

Rangvald read the skepticism in Ivar's face and his voice. He stepped forward and extended his arm. Ivar looked down at it before clasping his forearm in a warrior's handshake.

"You have my word as my brother's second-in-command and one day the captain of his warriors. If we can convince our fathers to end the feud on the promise that the next generation has already agreed to cease our hostility, perhaps Father can marry off Inga to someone else."

"And if that doesn't work, perhaps we suggest Signy instead. She is the older sister," Sven suggested.

"No," Harold and Rangvald responded at once.

"We keep our seer and healer," Harold barked.

"Besides, she's in love with Torbin. And she has cast her own runes. She knows her future lies with him." Rangvald voiced his opinion, too. There was a tightness around his eyes and mouth as though there was more to say, but he held back. Ivar nodded but did not press.

The three brothers finished caring for their horses, and the men had already been in the stables long enough to make Soren and Thor wonder what kept them. The men made their way to the bathhouse where Soren and Thor were already soaking in steaming tubs, guards from each tribe keeping an eye on the two feuding jarls and each other. Ivar and the other new arrivals stripped down and entered their own tubs.

"Ahh," Harold sighed. "My arse fell asleep those last ten miles or so, and I reek of horse shite. It's good to take a bath."

Rangvald splashed water at his older brother and laughed.

"You always smell of horse shite. If you didn't spend so much time in the stables rutting with the serving women and dairy maids, you might get rid of the stench."

Harold opened his mouth to respond, but snapped it shut as he reached for the soap. His one remaining hand worked the soap into a lather. He focused on bathing rather than a rejoinder. Sven's eyes darted back and forth between his brothers. While Harold had admitted Lorna's defense and losing his hand were fair parts of battle, he still harbored anger towards Rangvald for claiming Lorna as his. The fact that the couple had fallen in love left Harold without a hand or a bed slave. He had mentioned that once before and saw his life flash before his eyes when Rangvald nearly beat him to death. The three brothers now avoided conversation about Rangvald's personal relationships.

"The ceremony shall be in the morning," Soren announced as he watched Ivar's reaction.

Ivar's hands fisted under the water as his jaw ticked, but he said nothing. "We will exchange the dowry at the evening meal and announce the ceremony to the tribe," his father finished.

"Father," Rangvald spoke up. "Don't you think Mother and Inga would appreciate a little more time to recover from the journey and prepare for the ceremony?"

"That may be, but Jarl Soren and I have agreed that allying with a consummated marriage is more important than either your mother or your sister's gentle sensibilities."

"But I doubt Ivar would appreciate a bride who's too tired to remain awake on her wedding night," Harold spoke up.

Thor squinted at his sons and turned his head towards Soren, but his eyes were slow to follow. He nodded before looking at Soren. "Perhaps my sons have a point. We can exchange the dowry and documents this eve, but the ceremony can take place the day after tomorrow."

Soren grunted as his mouth tightened into a thin line, his ire directed at Ivar, somehow deducing that Harold and Rangvald were coming to Ivar's defense more than they were Inga's.

"Father, what type of ceremony will it be, since this is but a trial?" Sven relied on his age to mask the question in innocence when he intended to remind the two jarls that it was not a marriage in truth.

Both jarls' heads snapped toward Sven, and his eyes opened wide in true fear.

"The kind that solidifies an alliance that ends years of feuding. That's the kind," snarled Thor.

"But we all recognize that Harold, Rangvald, and Ivar get along better than any of the past jarls and their heirs. Perhaps they've already ended the feud." Sven kept his eyes down as he lathered his body and spoke at the same time.

"That doesn't make any lasting bond like marriage does, Sven. The bond of blood through our shared grandchildren is what will make the alliance last."

"Does that mean you think my brothers and Ivar won't honor--"

"Enough!" Thor roared as he stood from his bath. "Speak another word, Sven, and you will find yourself on a lonely horse back to our homestead."

"Ask Signy then. She already knows." Sven shot

his father a mutinous glare before sinking into the water to wet his hair.

"Sven, I warned you."

"Wait," Soren held up his hand. "What do you mean ask Signy? She has the second sight. Has she seen the future?"

Thor and his sons looked everywhere but at Ivar or Soren. They would not even look at one another. Their guilt seemed to ooze from them as Thor toweled himself dry, and the sons continued to scrub their bodies and hair.

"Thor?" Soren's voice held an edge of warning. "What has Signy seen?"

"Nothing of importance. She sees herself in love with one of my warriors. She says they will have a daughter that will marry your grandson. Nothing much more than that."

"Marry my grandson? So she would marry her cousin? And what do you mean nothing much more? That means something more."

"She believes her daughter will have her gift, too." Thor pulled on the clean clothes he brought with him and turned his attention to his sons. "Finish your baths and shake a leg. You don't want to keep our hosts waiting to serve the midday meal."

With a quick nod to Soren, Thor slipped from the bathhouse, having foregone the dip in the frigid water in the adjoining room. The hot water for the baths came from a natural hot spring beneath the building while the cold bath came from a rerouted portion of the fjord. The remaining five men moved to the cold pool and plunged in. No one spoke as the frigid water took their breath away. No one lingered either, all of them hurrying back into the steamy, heated room. They dressed in silence until Soren clapped his hand on Ivar's shoulder and blocked the only door.

"Harold, what else has Signy said about Ivar and Inga's marriage? Your father is leaving something out. He assumes you won't tell me. If there's a secret I should be aware of, but no one tells me, the alliance is off."

Harold and Rangvald exchanged a silent look then crossed their arms. They held the secret to what Signy had seen, and if it meant keeping Inga from marrying Ivar, an ally they already had, then they would risk their father's wrath. Neither of the current jarls would live forever. The agreements Harold, Rangvald, and Ivar made with each other would last longer than either of their fathers would.

"So that is how it is to be? You intend to sabotage the alliance your father and I have spent months working on. I shall be interested to see how he reacts to that piece of news. Sven might not be so lonely on that ride home after all."

Rangvald and Harold both dropped their arms. The older man had played them both. Rather than gain information, Soren would remove any detractors. He would clear the path to Ivar's wedding, taking names of new enemies as he went.

Ivar looked at Rangvald, Harold, and Sven as his father stormed out of the bathhouse.

"Well, that didn't go as we might have hoped," Ivar's dry tone filled the steam room with sarcasm. "Now there is no chance that my father will back down."

"Have Signy cast the runes before Father and Jarl Soren. Then what will they do? No one can deny Signy's gift. They would make fools of themselves if they did. We need only have enough witnesses that they cannot deny it." Sven looked at the older men and shrugged.

Rangvald wrapped his arm around his younger brother and pulled him against his side.

"Perhaps being the youngest has forced you to be the quietest, but it has given you the wisdom to watch and think. You may be the strategist of us all."

"I wouldn't go that far," Harold scoffed. "The boy barely has any hair on his chin and hasn't led a raid yet. Let us see his strategy when his life depends on it."

"It may very well if Father intends to send me home alone. With no marriage yet, Soren's men may murder me along the path, my body never to be seen again."

A shiver crept along Ivar's spine at Sven's observation. He suspected the young man spoke more truth than any of them wanted to accept.

NINE

Ivar entered the gathering hall within his family's longhouse and scanned the crowd for Lena. He always did, but this time when he spotted her, his heart pinched instead of leaped. He could not join her as she sat with her father and brother. Ivar had to join his parents at the head table where they entertained Thor's family. He noticed they had left a seat empty next to Inga. His stomach soured, and he was no longer interested in eating. He wanted to sit with Lena, wrap his arm around her waist, and whisper how he planned for them to spend their night. With Inga at the homestead, there was next to no chance that Lena would meet him. Even if he could not make love to her, he longed to be sure she was faring well and not feeling abandoned. He already knew the truth to both thoughts. She would not be doing well, and it was impossible for her not to feel abandoned. Ivar just did not have any solutions.

He watched as Signy left the head table and wove through the crowd to sit next to a young man who was at the far end of the table where Lena and her family sat. It did not take long for Ivar to realize that the young man must have been the one mentioned earlier. Torbin. Signy nudged Torbin further down the bench to make it appear as though he made room for her, but Ivar realized she did it to sit closer to Lena. He did not doubt that Signy told Torbin to sit at that table, so she joined him without directly approaching Lena. Ivar's curiosity nagged at him to discover what Signy would tell Lena and what she had already learned.

Instead of going to the head table, Ivar worked his way through the crowd, greeting his men and nodding to Thor's. He found Vigo and Eindride and dipped his head towards Lena. They met each other behind Lena's back and looked engrossed in conversation, but the three of them strained to hear the conversation taking place at the table.

"Don't worry." Ivar caught Signy's voice.

"How can I not? I should have seized the chance to say goodbye. Now it's just over." Ivar wanted to pull Lena into his arms and carry her away, promising that nothing was over. But he could not.

"Won't marry." Ivar against only heard a snippet of Signy's comment. He had no way of knowing who she meant. Did she mean he and Lena would not marry? Or could it be that Ivar and Inga would not? Or perhaps she was talking about someone else.

"You need to go to your family," hissed Eindride. "Your father looks ready to murder you."

"After the conversation in the bathhouse, despite me barely saying anything at all, he might. But not until after he gets her dowry," Ivar muttered.

"Go. I'll stay and listen."

Ivar nodded and made his way to the chair his family and guests saved for him. Inga barely spared him a glance. He followed Inga's line of sight and realized she was staring at Lena's back.

"Had to check on your precious lover?" Inga's did not bother to lower her voice. "You just had to be near her? Did you catch her scent like a dog in heat?"

Before Ivar responded, and he had not planned to, Inga yelped, and the table rattled. Rangvald sat across from her, and he had clearly kicked her under the table.

"Don't be the only bitch here, Inga," Rangvald murmured. "Test your groom's patience before he's even bedded you, and you might find marriage to be far rougher than you expect."

Rangvald cocked an eyebrow, making the insinuation that Ivar might abuse her all the clearer. Inga's face set in a mask of fury, and her body went rigid. Rangvald chuckled and shook his head.

"You won't be the prized daughter of a jarl here. You won't even be frú yet. Perhaps you should remember you catch more flies with honey than vinegar. Your face looks drier than a pickled herring in December. I would have a care, Inga. Once we leave, there will be no one here who has to like you." Rangvald shoveled a large bite of stew into his mouth and still managed a wolfish grin.

Inga remained silent for the rest of the meal as the conversation flowed around her. Rangvald did not spare his sister another glance, but Lorna, who sat to Rangvald's left, took surreptitious glances at Inga. She understood the woman better than her brothers did. She would wait until the end of the meal, then she would warn Lena that she needed to leave the homestead and not ask for anyone's help except for those she trusted the most.

As soon as Lorna managed to slip away, she searched for Lena outside. Ivar and Lena had helped her when she sought refuge months ago. She was duty bound to return the favor, and she liked Lena. They had become friends in the short time Lorna stayed with them, and she would do what she could to protect her friend.

"Lena," Lorna's whisper hissed through the air. "Lena!"

Lena paused, looking back over her shoulder as the hair on her neck prickled. She spotted Lorna waving for her to stop. Lorna dashed across the distance that separated them and pulled Lena towards Lena's home.

"Shh," Lorna warned. "Dinna say anything yet. I canna tell who can hear."

When they entered Lena's home, Lorna did a sweep through the chambers until it satisfied her that no one was hiding.

"What're you doing? There's no one home but us. My father has gone to visit his companion, and my brother is in the mead hall thinking he has a far higher tolerance than he does. I just hope he doesn't come home with another black eye and broken fingers."

"There's nay one here this time, but I'm nae confident that there willna be someone lying in wait one of these days." Lorna took Lena's hands and drew her to sit before the fire. "Inga is dangerous. Her brothers dinna see it, but I do. She and Ulfhild are nae women to underestimate. They may nae wield swords, but they are manipulative and have learned how to make men do their begging. Inga in particular. At least ten of the guards who traveled with us receive favors from her in return for spying for her."

Lorna cocked an eyebrow at Lena as the latter looked at Lorna askance. It was no great shock that Inga might not be a virgin, but Lena worried for Ivar's safety if she set ten men against him.

"Ye're worrying about Ivar's wellbeing, but it's yer safety ye should fear for. Lena, I'm serious. Inga is plotting something. I'm nae sure what yet. But I watched her throughout the meal. She seethed after Rangvald humiliated her in front of Ivar. He basically said Ivar would beat her or take her roughly if she didna start being sweeter. She canna do anything to Rangvald, and she doesnae dare do anything to Ivar. But she will take out her anger on you."

"How can you be so sure? She knows who I am, but there are still laws about attacking free women."

"Because she's tried it on me. She had some of her lackies attack me one day just after I'd left the sparring ring. Rangvald was on a hunt, and none of the women like me enough to come to my aid. I could fight them off, but nae before they banged me up. I lied to Rangvald and told him missing him distracted me while I practiced, and I received my comeuppance for it. I defended myself well enough that none of her men will risk taking me on. And, to be honest, Rangvald hasnae left me alone long enough. I think he suspects more than I told him, but he hasnae pressed."

"What are you suggesting? I can't tell Ivar any of this. He would never leave my side. I can't ask you and Rangvald to protect me, or Jarl Thor would tell Jarl Soren I'm trying to cause trouble. Eindride won't keep a secret from Ivar. And I sure don't trust Harold, and Sven is just too young. My brother is too young. My father is still strong enough to work the fields and fight one or two men, but he would die before he fended off ten men. Even Ivar or Rangvald would."

"I will speak to Rang tonight. We can keep Inga occupied and with either Signy or me until the wedding. Once they are bound by the trial marriage, it will give Inga more freedom than any of us can control. Leave then. Find someone who can take ye away. It doesnae have to be forever, but it does have to be until Ivar can prove the marriage is a disaster."

"Eindride has to be the one then. I intended on asking him to take me Kaupang where I could live once Ivar married. Ivar trusts him, and if Ivar knows it's not forever, he will let Eindride take me. If Inga believes I'm leaving for good, then she might not care if you and Rangvald accompany us. Or if she minds, she won't be able to kill me as easily while we travel."

"Speak to Eindride as soon as ye can. This canna wait. Ye canna go to Ivar, and he canna come to ye. Eindride will have to be yer go-between. Perhaps people will see ye with Eindride and think Ivar has passed ye along. That is the best that ye can hope for until we can get ye away. Pack tonight and be ready to go as soon as the ceremony is over."

Lorna pulled Lena in for a tight embrace, and both women savored the moment, neither having had sisters.

Lorna tucked hair behind Lena's ear before hugging her again.

"I only had brothers, and they died before they could marry. I already love Signy as a sister, but I am so glad to have ye as well. I think one day blood shall connect our families. It will be yers that courses through our grandchildren."

"Do you believe that?"

"I do, and I havenae even asked Signy."

"Do you have the gift of sight?"

Lorna chuckled. "Nae in the least. If I had, my family would be alive. And if I had, then I would have realized without so much heartache that Rang feels the same aboot me as I do aboot him. I just have the strongest feeling that I can't shake. We will be a family one day. More than once over, I am sure."

Lena walked Lorna to the door and peered out before Lorna stepped into the brisk autumn air.

"There's Eindride," Lena murmured. "Send him to me, and I can explain everything tonight."

Lorna looked around before sprinting to Eindride who appeared to be headed to the mead hall. Lena watched as Lorna was brief before tilting her head in Lena's direction. Eindride nodded and stepped around Lorna. His frame blocked Lena's view of Lorna. She waited at the door until he reached her. Lena moved aside and allowed Eindride in. She breathed a sigh of relief that they had been friends since they were both toddlers.

"What's going on, Lena? Lorna said it was urgent that I see you. You need my protection, but she wouldn't say why. She said no one can see her talking to me for too long and that you would explain."

"Lorna came to warn me about Inga. She's already been on the receiving end of Inga's threats, and she fears Inga will take action to make sure I don't live long enough to tempt Ivar."

"Inga has never swung a sword in her life. I doubt she even knows what to do with a knife." Eindride crossed his arms, and his smug expression made Lena want to slap him.

"She might not, but she has at least ten of her guardsmen who will act on her behalf. She has arrangements with them." Lena paused to let that set in. "Ein, I wanted you to take me to Kaupang before Ivar marries, but he refused when I brought it up. Now, with Lorna's warning, I have little choice. Inga had some of her men attack Lorna while Rangvald was away hunting. Apparently, they bashed her about enough for Rangvald to question what happened. She didn't tell him, but she believes he's guessed. Ein, take me to Kaupang at least long enough for Ivar to prove the marriage is a sham. With me not here, no one can say I'm tempting him away. Lorna said she and Rangvald might to ride with us."

"No," Eindride shook his head emphatically. "Absolutely not. Ivar will lose his mind if you disappear. No."

"I didn't say we would hide this from him. You have to be the one to explain. I can't take the chance of being seen with him. Please, Ein. If not for my sake, then for Ivar's. He has to at least try with Inga, or everything will fall apart. And who will people blame? Not Ivar. Not Inga. Not Jarl Soren. Me. I'll be to blame."

Eindride paused for a long moment, but Lena saw when he capitulated. She embraced him, but before she said thank you, the door burst open with a roar so loud, Lena thought it was a bear.

Ivar watched Lorna speaking to Eindride and wondered why his friend's woman was speaking to his other friend. Then his heart rate spiked when Eindride looked around as if to make sure no one was watching him and walked to Lena's door. He watched Lena waiting for Eindride at the door and welcoming him with a smile. Eindride had not visited Lena alone in her home since before Ivar became involved with her. Or so he thought.

Ivar watched, expecting Eindride's departure at any moment, but as the minutes ticked by, his suspicious fears created a choke hold. Could his best friend be having an affair with the one woman he loved? Part of his mind chided him for the ridiculousness of the thought while the other part clamored for him to run Eindride through and carry Lena away. His emotions already overwrought with fear that Lena was slipping away, or rather being pulled away, because of his impending wedding.

When Eindride made no sign of leaving Lena's longhouse, Ivar stormed across the village green and took a breath before kicking open the door. He roared when he saw Lena standing in the center of the room embracing Eindride. Ivar launched himself at Eindride before asking questions. He knocked Eindride to the floor, tackling him as his fist raised to slam into his face, but before he landed the first punch, Eindride looked away.

"Gods, Lena!" Eindride yelled.

Ivar looked over and saw Lena lying on the floor next to the table, a gash on her forehead from where she must have hit the corner when Ivar's attack knocked her over as well. Ivar scrambled off Eindride and crawled to Lena's side.

"Lena," his voice cracked. He looked back at Eindride. "I killed her."

"I'm not dead, but I'm angrier than a shaken hive. Help me up." Lena hissed as she tried to push herself into a sitting position.

"No, wait." Ivar choked out. He scooped Lena into his arms and carried her to a chair before the fire. He was cautious when he nestled her against his chest as he lowered himself into the chair. "Ein, get a wet cloth."

Ivar crooned nonsensical words to Lena as he pressed the cold compress against the cut on her forehead. Once he cleared away the initial blood, he realized that it was not as deep as he feared.

"I'm sorry, Lena. So, so sorry."

"Why'd you come crashing in here like a bear woken from a nap? Why'd you go for Ein?" Lena's voice was raspy, but her eyes were clear and focused. Ivar was thankful for small blessings.

"I--" Ivar looked over his shoulder at Eindride, his guilt obvious to anyone. He hung his head before muttering. "I saw Eindride come in here, and then he stayed for so long that I became suspicious. I'm sorry, Ein."

"You thought I'd betray you?" Lena gasped.

"You thought I would take what is yours? We are like brothers, but we have never shared like that." Ivar knew he warranted Eindride's indignation.

"You were speaking to Lorna who had just come from here, then you looked around as though expecting someone to catch you, then you stayed in here for so long."

"So long?" Lena interjected. "He was here five minutes. You assumed I would turn away from you that fast. And with your best friend. Let go of me. Leave, Ivar."

Lena tried to push away and almost fell to the floor. She stood up so suddenly that the room spun, and she covered her mouth as her supper threatened to revisit her. Ivar wrapped his arm around her shoulder and turned her against his chest. Once Lena was sure she would not be ill, she stepped away.

"Leave, Ivar."

"What? No, I'm not leaving you alone when you're hurt. I'll at least wait until Tormud returns."

"No. I don't want to be near you right now. I don't need a nursemaid."

"And I'm not leaving you alone with a head injury. I'll wait out here if you retire to your chamber."

"I don't want to retire right now. And I damn well don't want you here!" Lena grasped her head as her voice reverberated through her skull. "Get out. I wouldn't have a head injury if you weren't jealous and arrogant."

"And I want to fix it."

"Go see your bride. Fix that."

Ivar jerked back as though Lena struck him. He shook his head, then looked at Eindride, who stepped toward the door.

"Lena, tell him what we were talking about. Forgive him for being an ass or not, but you have to tell him. You think this was bad." Eindride pretended to shiver as he pulled the door open and stepped out, closing the door behind him.

"Tell me what?"

"Nothing that can't wait until morning when I'm not so angry with you."

"I've apologized, and I feel wretched for hurting you and assuming the worst. Gods, Lena. Don't you think I fear you will find someone else rather than wait for me to sort out this mess with Inga? I thought I was watching my greatest fear come to life before my eyes. I thought you'd already moved on. And I'm not sure if thinking it was Eindride made it worse or better. Worse since he's my best friend, but better knowing he would care for you properly."

"You are an idiot. Eindride would never touch me. He's too loyal to you for starters, and Brenna would never look at him again. He's never wanted me. He's had his eye on Brenna for years, but she was too young. You can't see anything around you. How will you ever lead?" Lena's eyes opened wide as she realized what her words meant. "I'm sorry. That was uncalled for. I shouldn't have said that, Ivar. Everyone knows you're already the real leader, not your father."

"You didn't say anything untrue. Where you're concerned, I can't see beyond needing you." Ivar inched towards Lena and waited to see if she would pull away. When she remained rooted to where she stood, he raised his arms. She stepped into his embrace and rested the uninjured size of her head against his chest. "What was Eindride saying about something you need to tell me."

"It's what he and I were talking about before you stormed in. You saw me embracing a friend willing to go out of his way to help me, help us. Lorna worries that Inga will lash out at me. She has good reason to believe Inga has guardsmen at her beck and call. She's trading her favors to have them on her side. Inga had some men attack Lorna a while ago when Rangvald was away.

"Lorna fears Inga will have me killed, or at best, hurt," Lena continued. "She thinks Ein should take me away until you can end things. Lorna thinks if we leave after the ceremony, Inga will just be glad to see the back of me. Inga might leave me alone if she thinks I won't be competition for her. Lorna said she and Rangvald could accompany us, and that would offer me another layer of protection."

"Where would you go?" Ivar thought he might cry for the first time since he was seven and his brothers stole and broke his wooden sword.

"Kaupang like I planned. I have family there, and there's work, too."

"How long?" Ivar's throat felt like it was held in a vice.

"Until you can end the trial marriage and Inga goes home."

"And if I can't end things?" Ivar whispered.

"Then there wouldn't be any point in me being here, anyway."

"There is always a point to you being here."

"Not if we have to see each other but can't talk, can't touch, can't love each other. No. Neither of us wants that."

"But don't you think remaining here would drive Inga away faster? If she doesn't feel threatened, then she might become comfortable here. What if she doesn't want to go home once she thinks she's won?"

Lena shook her head against his chest before burrowing further into his embrace.

"I don't know," came her muffled reply. "Maybe

you're right. But I don't want to wait and fear when the attack will inevitably come. You can't assign a guard to me. Your father would never allow it, and it would infuriate Jarl Thor. It would be a slight to Inga, showing everyone that you value me above her. You can't expect Ein to just follow me around, nor can Rang or Lorna do it."

"But if we make people think you moved on to Ein, then perhaps it would ease some tension."

"No. It would devastate Brenna, and we don't dare tell her. We can't risk too many people knowing any plan we decide on."

"If Ein trusts her enough to want to marry her, then she may be an asset to making this believable. She plays the role of the jilted lover. She makes it easier for people to believe Ein swept in once I ended things with you."

Lena shook her head. "I don't want people believing I'm the whore Inga claims. To move on so quickly, and to your best friend. To your second-in-command as if I'm after the most powerful man I can seduce. I'd rather leave and not have to see you with her, not have to be reminded that she sleeps beside you every night. That you are joining with her."

"That will never happen," Ivar bellowed.

"But it has to."

"No, it doesn't. No one can make me stick my cock where I don't want it to go."

"Your father can if he insists on witnessing you bedding her."

"No. I will say I won't dishonor my wife by having anyone watch us. Then I will swear her to silence."

"Swear Inga to silence? You have better luck convincing Loki to be honest. She will defy you just for the sake of being awkward."

"Not if she believes Rangvald's threat."

"You would threaten Inga with violence to make her obey. Ha." Lena's laugh was hollow. "She's more likely to kill you in your sleep."

"Can we compromise? We try my plan with you pretending to be Ein's companion, and if that doesn't work, then Ein takes you to Kaupang."

"And if I don't live long enough to leave later?"

"Ein and I can be discreet when we set our most trusted men to guard you. They can follow you at a distance that doesn't make it obvious. I can have more than one set on duty, so they can switch depending on where you are in the village. That keeps it from making anyone suspicious or alerting them. They'll just look like they're moving through the village as normal, going about their business. Rangvald and Harold can deal with their own men who give their fealty to Inga rather than their father."

Lena inhaled as she considered what Ivar suggested. As she decided, she exhaled.

"Fine. We can try it, but if she threatens me, I will kill the men who attack me, and I will leave."

"If you're harmed, or if anyone attempts to, I would never forgive myself. No one is getting close enough to you to try."

"I hope you're right."

TEN

Inga watched Ivar run across the village green before storming into Lena's longhouse. She seethed as she watched her husband return to his lover. The blessing may not have been done yet, but as far as she was concerned, their marriage began when their fathers signed the papers. The man owed his loyalty and devotion to her. The longer Ivar remained in Lena's home, the more convinced Inga became that she would need to relieve herself of the competition.

"Inga, what are you doing standing out here. It's getting cold."

Inga turned around to the voice of a young man. Her attention riveted to his hazel eyes and the strong jawline. He could not have been much older than her at sixteen, but he had the body of a young warrior. Her nostrils flared as he approached, and she smelled fresh pine and soap.

"Who are you?" Inga whispered as the man came to stand so close that their toes touched.

"Einar."

"Just Einar?"

"For now."

"And what will I call you later?"

"Your lover."

Inga gasped and stepped back. While it instantly attracted her to the young man, she had not expected him to be so brash so soon. She shook her head and took another step back.

"You are far too presumptuous. Why would I ever take you as a lover when I am wed to the jarl's son? Who are you but a warrior and the son of a warrior?"

"I am a warrior, but my father is a farmer." Einar grinned as he admitted his father's social status was even lower than she had assumed. While it was not true, she did not need to know that yet. He would test her to see whether her attraction would outweigh her snobbery. "However, I am a man who has already heard about the things you enjoy, and I can offer that and far more to you. Your father's men will leave, and that will leave you needy. Ivar will never fuck you the way you want. That leaves me."

"Why? Is it because of my position? The power I will have?"

Einar stepped forward until he backed Inga into the shadows of the building. He bracketed her head with his forearms and leaned in so close to her ear, Inga wondered if he might kiss her neck.

"I don't care about your power. You will have none until Soren dies, and he is a man in his prime. What I want is my cock inside you. What I want is to hear you call my name as I pleasure you. If what I can see with your clothes on is any hint to what you look like without them, then I will be the luckiest man in this tribe."

"You want to take what is not yours. What belongs to the jarl's heir. You are bold to approach me. How can you be sure I won't run and tell Ivar or my father or even Jarl Soren?"

"Because I saw your reaction as I approached. I

hear the way your breath hitches. I believe I can even smell your arousal. I would wager if I stuck my fingers in your sheath, I'll find you're already soaking wet for me. Would I be wrong?"

"No," Inga breathed on a sigh. Her eyes darted around to ensure no one could see them. "Prove to me you are worth it."

Einar captured her mouth in a punishing kiss, nipping at her bottom lip before swiping his tongue beyond her teeth. He pulled back long enough to demand, "Suck it."

Inga was only too happy to oblige. As Einar's tongue thrust forward again, she drew it further into her mouth, applying enough pressure that it should hurt. Einar pressed his arousal against her mons as he squeezed her breast without mercy. His other hand began raising her skirts as she struggled with the laces of his leather pants.

"My tongue is only a hint of what I will do to you tonight. You shall suck my cock later, but for now, I will drive it into your quim until you explode. You are mine, Inga."

The forcefulness of his tone made Inga's core ache. While she was a demanding young woman, she longed for a man who would dominate her. She had to pay guardsmen to couple with her the way she wanted. Even the roughest of warriors did not meet her needs. She suspected Einar might. Einar spun her around and pressed her breasts against the log wall of the storage building they ducked behind. He ran his hand over one of her bottom cheeks before digging his fingers into the meaty flesh. She had an ample backside, and he spread her cheeks wide.

"By the end of tonight, Inga, there will not be a part of you that isn't mine."

Einar grasped her hips and impaled her with his rod. What he was not about to admit was Inga was the first woman he ever joined with, that this was the first time anything more than his hand had pleasured his cock. He thrust over and over, pressing her against the building. His need for release driving him to a frenzy, testing the little control he had, but he refused to finish so fast that he embarrassed himself. He had sensed what Inga needed long before he approached her. She was a spoiled woman who needed a man to master her. She tested every man she came across, seeming to hope to find one who would rise to the challenge. Not only did he desire her, but he desired the power being her lover would bring. Being the lover of the future frú would grant him access and information he would not gain even with his brother Eindride being Ivar's closest friend. The access he desired was to Lena. He would settle for Inga as his lover for now, but he would prove to Lena that he could satisfy her far better than Ivar ever could.

Inga moaned as Einar continued to push her body harder against the wall. Being trapped between the hard wall and the hard planes of Einar's body excited her. When one of her moans was too loud, he wrapped his fingers around her threat and murmured beside her ear.

"Don't make me silence you, Inga. No one can find out about this. Do you want me to stop?" He pulled out and grinned when she whimpered.

"No," she pleaded.

Once more he thrust into her, pushing her cheek flush against the wall, his fingers biting once more into her backside.

"Remember who fucks you the best, Inga. If I find out you are still returning to your guardsmen, I will not be thrilled. I will punish you."

"Punish me?"

"Yes. Deny you my cock. Spank you. Tie you to my bed while I tease your quim but refuse to bring you release. You consented to be my lover, and now your body is mine. I don't share."

"Yes, Einar. Yes." Inga panted as his words along with his cock brought her to release. Einar covered her mouth with his hand as she moaned once more. He no longer held back and flooded her with his seed.

"It will be my children you carry. It will be my sons who one day rule this tribe. I will keep you pregnant so often Ivar's seed will never take root." Einar pressed all of his weight against her, making it impossible for Inga to move. "Do you understand our arrangement?"

Inga struggled but nodded. Einar removed his hand from her mouth but tangled it in her hair, tugging hard.

"Is it what you want?"

"Gods, yes. Einar, I'll do anything you want. Please just keep doing this." Inga's mind fractured between the desperation to experience Einar's coupling again and disgust that she did not hesitate to submit. It was as though he cast a spell over her when he approached, and she had no strength or reason to fight against it. She had never given in to a man so easily, but something deep within demanded she submitted over and over. She could not piece through it, but then she did not really want to.

"I intend to. You will retire now and make your parents believe you are asleep. I will come to your window in an hour, and you will let me in. I have a cock that needs sucking, and you have an arse that needs my attention." Einar eased the pressure on her hair and stepped back far enough to turn Inga to face him. He stroked her cheek as he feathered kisses along her other cheek. "Have you given your arse to another man?"

Inga shook her head. Einar leaned in and gave

Inga such a tender kiss she grasped the front of his tunic and clung to him. The kiss was gentle and loving after what they had just experienced.

"That's good to know, my little one. That is one part of you I am sure I will not have to share with Ivar."

"I wish you didn't have to share any part with him," Inga admitted. "How can I ever give myself to another man when I know what you will give me? You understand what I want, what I need. How is that even possible?"

"I do understand, Inga, and I will be your lover for the rest of our lives." With another gentle kiss but a punishing twist of her nipple, Einar stepped out of her reach. "Go to your chamber and ready yourself for me. I expect you to be naked when I arrive."

"Yes, Einar." Inga's complete capitulation stirred Einar's cock once more. He was not even sure how he gained such influence over her with such ease.

"You will come to love me beyond reason one day, Inga. And I will give you everything your body desires." Einar spun on his heel and walked away, leaving Inga staring at his retreating, aroused once more to the point where the ache in her core burned.

Einar could not believe how simple it had been to seduce Inga. He had to admit to himself that most of what he said was true. Einar would command her body; he would pleasure her in ways he understood she needed, but no other man would give her; he would plant his seed to take root over and over; and she would fall in love with him. Or at least she would believe she was in love with him once he made her solely dependent upon him for both her physical and emotional needs. Einar would use his position to get closer to Lena when he suggested to Inga things that she should demand of Ivar. He would convince Ivar that as the younger brother of his best friend, no one was more trustworthy to watch over Lena. He would convince Inga that it was so he could plant seeds of doubt and distrust with Lena, telling her how Ivar loved Inga more. Once he did that, Lena would never continue with Ivar. She would be free for him to marry. Lena might carry the children born from his love for her, but his children born of Inga would one day rule this tribe. He just had to have patience for a little longer, and he would have the woman he had fantasized about since the first time he palmed himself.

Inga stood watching Einar until he entered the mead hall. She leaned against the wall as tears streamed down her cheeks. Inga had never given into a man so quickly. She had plenty of men pursue her, and she pursued the ones she wanted. But never had a man completely captivated her to the point where all she did was beg to surrender. For the first time since learning she would marry Ivar, she regretted the arrangement. There was no way out of it, and there was no way her father would ever let her marry a man like Einar, but that did not mean she could not accept his offer. She was sure she was already halfway in love with him.

ELEVEN

"You must go," Lena murmured, even though she had not released her hold on Ivar's waist. "Inga will have a fit if she learns you came here tonight."

"Inga doesn't control me. I am not married to her yet. Where I go will always be my business, and right now, I am here and am not going anywhere else." Ivar brushed hair away from the cut on her forehead and kissed just beside it. "Let me tend to you tonight. I'll bathe you and put you to bed, where I will spend the night loving you."

"Is this your way of saying goodbye?" Lena choked out the words.

"Never. There will never be a goodbye. Not in this life or the next."

"Gods, I hope so. Ivar, I keep trying to tell myself I can give you up, that I can make a life without you, but I don't think I can. What will I do without you? It would be like I lost half of me. The desperation is choking me, even while I try to convince you it's best for us to part. I can't shake the constant fear that fate will separate us."

"I know, my love. I feel it, too. But we will begin our plan tomorrow. For now, I am here to make love to you and remind you I am always yours. Let me gather the hot water." Ivar released her, but she rested her hand on his arm.

"Only if you bathe with me," she murmured.

The wolfish grin that was Ivar's only response made Lena's core clench and her breath hitch. Four years, and there was no sign that Lena's reaction to Ivar would ever diminish. It was visceral, raw, innate. He had drawn her like he was a loadstone since they were children, but it had been the same with Eindride. They had been the best of friends, but as they matured and their desires for companionship shifted from those of childhood, Lena had always known her feelings for Ivar differed from those toward any other man. It had only taken a drunken night for them to lower their inhibitions. A single kiss at the taunting of their friends had altered their relationship forever. What was meant to be a brushing of the lips or even an exaggerated and sloppy farce morphed in an instant to something that all those around them recognized was combustible. They left the mead hall without a word or a glance to anyone else. It was not a romantic first time for either of them. It was a joining against the side of a building that answered a call they both had ignored. It was a joining that forever altered the course they imagined they would follow, but one the gods had ordained. Or at least fate led them to believe that for the past four years. Now it felt as though it had only been Loki the trickster who had a hand in their relationship, a hand that taunted and manipulated. rather than a nurturing nudge from the goddess Freyja.

Ivar pulled the tub from where it rested on its side and moved throughout the longhouse, setting pails of water before the fire to warm and gathering soap and drying linens. All the items he found with ease after many nights of bathing at Lena's, many nights of bathing with Lena. His cock twitch against the tight seam of his leather pants. He ached to release it from its confines and find relief within Lena. It took little effort to remember what it was like to slide into the only woman he had desired. He had loved her as all childhood friends did one another, but when his body began to stir with needs for release, it was only ever Lena who he pictured, wanted. It was the sight, the sound, the smell of her that would stir him to taking himself in hand night after night. The pressure from friends to kiss her had been the excuse he had longed for since the first time his cock hardened because of her. The first time he entered her, he was convinced there would be no one else. It was as though his need both intensified and satisfied in that moment when they came together and finally became the singular entity that made them both stronger, happier, better. The thought of being forced to couple with Inga made him furious and nauseous all at once. He wanted to scream each time someone mentioned it, since he attempted to avoid thinking about it. He already realized he could not go through with it, though they might force him to try.

"Do you think we will have long before Tormud and Jan return?"

"Father has gone to visit Astrid, so he'll be away for the night. Jan will return drunk and unsatisfied. I can assure you he will go directly to his chamber." Lena's grin made Ivar chuckle.

"Poor boy. I remember those days."

"Oh?" Lena cocked an eyebrow, not sure she appreciated Ivar's empathy toward her brother.

Ivar pulled Lena into his arms as he loosened her braid, running his fingers through the tresses that fell to her waist. "Oh yes. I remember how my cock ached until I returned to my chamber and ease my need for you. You were the bane of my existence and the fulfillment of my dreams all wrapped into one agonizingly beautiful package. Now that I know you love me and I can feast upon you whenever I want, you are just the fulfillment of my dreams."

"For me?" Lena's lips turned down in a mocking frown as her fingers worked the laces at the neck of Ivar's tunic.

"Yes, for you. You know that you were the reason I would take swims in the freezing fjord, woke up in the middle of the night to a cock that was still pulsing, and eased my suffering with my own hand."

"Eased your suffering? You have never suffered from anything but a cold. And that hasn't happened in years."

Ivar lifted Lena's dress over her head, tossing it aside as he gazed at her body. He pressed her hand against the ridge within his pants, groaning when she took command alternating squeezing and stroking.

"How I suffer now, my little seductress."

"I cannot bear the thought of causing your agony. Let me ease that suffering." Lena finished unlacing Ivar's pants and pushed them down over his hips before sinking to her knees. Lena cupped his bollocks before looking up from under her lashes. She pressed her breasts together, surrounding his rod with the mounds of flesh. She bent her head towards him and licked the tip each time he thrust.

Ivar's hand braced her shoulders as though he needed to support to remain on his feet. He watched as his rod moved between her breasts, momentarily disappearing before emerging to receive a kiss. He watched as Lena's eyes darkened and her pupils dilated with unspent desire. It only made his bollocks tighten as he raced towards completion. Lena read the signs, letting her breasts drop away as her mouth consumed him to the root. She relaxed and savored the power of knowing she drove Ivar to the brink of losing control. Lena had experienced the same eking away of her restraint countless times when Ivar worked his magic on her body. The first salty drops landed on her tongue, making her hum with delight. The vibration was more than Ivar could withstand. He pulled free and stroked himself until his seed sprayed across Lena's chest and breasts. His satisfaction was more than physical. He had marked her once more as his, seeing his seed upon her skin, knowing no other man had ever possessed such a privilege.

Lena rose to her feet and walked to the tub without looking back. She was certain Ivar would follow. She was unprepared for him to grasp her hand and spin her towards the large table upon which they took their meals. He pressed her against it as he slid his still hard cock between the cheeks of her backside.

"How am I still so hard?" he wondered aloud. "How can I still need you when you just gave me such pleasure?"

Ivar slid into her sheath, and they both moaned. His body draped over hers, their fingers interlocked on the table, him dropping a kiss behind her ear before sucking the lobe between his teeth.

"I know why," he continued. "I haven't pleasured you, my love."

"A pleasure you shall undoubtedly share, too," Lena teased.

"That is true, but there is plenty of time tonight when it will be your turn alone. Many, many times tonight."

He would be true to his word. She often wondered how she functioned on only a couple of hours of sleep each night. Ivar stayed with her every night that his father did not demand he return to the jarl's longhouse. Most nights they only managed two or three hours of sleep at best, both waking each other throughout the night. Ivar had tried to move Lena into his chamber permanently after Lorna left with Rangvald, but his father had been livid. Ivar solved the problem by returning to Lena's home instead.

"More, Ivar," Lena panted as Ivar's thrusts pressed her mound against the lip of the table. The sensation against her pearl and the feel of him within was catapulting her towards release. She threw back her head as sensation after sensation flowed through her like waves crashing across cliffs. Her body tensed, her muscles clenching, as she tried to prolong the sensations. Ivar rocked his hips against her backside as his own release filled her.

They moved, climbing into the tub, before positioning themselves so Lena's back pressed against Ivar's chest. They allowed the warm water to envelop them as they relaxed. The water was both soothing and erotic. Ivar's hand rested on Lena's belly, the touch both protective and possessive to each of them. His other hand kneaded her breast as her hands gripped his thighs. They had done this so many times that they had a routine. They would rest together before Ivar lathered soap to run over Lena's body. Then Lena would return the favor by turning to face Ivar. Their anticipation mounting with each swipe of the soap. They would wash one another's hair, Ivar having to lean far forward for Lena to rinse his with fresh water. It was an excuse for him to begin his feast on her breast. They would finish by slowly coupling as the water lapped about their chests. Neither wanted to consider this might be the last time they would enjoy the connection.

Once they finished, Ivar and Lena drained the tub and climbed into bed. While they normally chatted about the parts of their day they spent apart, that night they held one another until they drifted to sleep. However, without fail, their need for one another woke them throughout the night.

Ivar stretched as the first rays of morning crept through Lena's window. He rolled to pull Lena into his embrace, but his arms remained empty. Ivar looked about the room to find Lena standing at the window, the soft light casting a glow around her naked form. Ivar slipped from the bed and came to stand behind her, wrapping his arms around her middle. He felt her shudder, then tremble.

"Lena?" He attempted to turn Lena toward him, but she would not budge, shaking her head. Ivar did not pressure her, and in return, Lena relaxed against his body; however, her trembling did not cease. Ivar's heart broke as his one great love cried, knowing, even accepting, that they might say goodbye to their relationship and their connection that morning. "We have today. Let's go for a ride. We can spend the day together."

Lena shook her head and turned around. Ivar brushed the stream of tears from her cheeks, but the stain from the trail remained, a reminder to Ivar that despite Lena's constant attempt at stoicism, their circumstances deeply pained her.

"That's impossible. You must go before everyone realizes you didn't sleep in your chamber. For all we know, Inga tried to go to you last night, only to find you missing. She will not let that go unspoken. You must pay your court on her today. Tomorrow you will marry her."

Lena's tears began again as she turned away, but Ivar caught her in his embrace, her face resting against his chest. His warm skin and steady heartbeat were so familiar and comforting to Lena, and her tears devolved into sobs. Ivar stroked her hair while his own tears fell.

It was Lena's turn to absorb the trembles, and she leaned back to see the tears flowing from Ivar's hazel eyes. Their hearts broke all over again as they recognized their own pain mirrored in their lover. Lena reached up and brushed away Ivar's tears. Ivar cupped her jaw as their lips fused for the most tender kiss they had ever exchanged. It was slow as each of them poured their love into it, praying the other would absorb the love they each offered.

"I will make this work. You are and always will be the one great love of my life. You are who I need and want as my wife, my partner. You are the woman this tribe needs to one day help lead us. I will not give up on us."

"Patience." Lena sighed.

"Patience." Ivar kissed her forehead before they stepped apart and dressed for the day.

TWELVE

Ivar stepped into the dim light of the gathering hall. He looked about the many sleeping bodies, some having passed out where they sat, others stretched out with furs covering them. Ivar glanced toward the head table and found his father glaring at him. Ivar wanted to cringe, but there was no ignoring his father. He made his way toward the man who was his leader and father, both positions enabling him to command Ivar to his will.

"You insulted our guests last night." Soren did not waste words.

"Who followed me? Someone would have had to if you were sure I wasn't in my chamber."

"Your wife. She informed her father you were missing."

"And how would she if she hadn't either followed me or gone to my chamber? Neither of which are appropriate." Ivar scowled. "And she's not my wife."

"She will be by tonight."

Ivar stifled his grimace as he sat beside his father.

"The ceremony isn't until tomorrow."

"They have moved the *wedding* forward. At your wife's demand."

"Demand? That seems rather presumptuous for

someone who has been here less than a day. Already giving orders and not even blessed as your heir's wife. I wonder what other demands she intends to make, now that she knows our wills can get bent."

Soren growled as his knuckles turned white, his grip on his mug so tight that Ivar waited for it to crack.

"She is a woman on the eve of her wedding, and her husband is bedding another woman."

"And she intended to be bedded before the ceremony. I'm just not convinced I'm the one she wanted to fuck."

"How dare you speak of your wife in such a manner?"

"I dare because everyone knows she's fucking half the guards her father brought. I heard more than one person whispering such last night. I'll wager she insists some of the men remain after her family leaves. I bet she'll complain to her father that she isn't comfortable yet without familiar faces. Do you intend to have strange warriors, ones trained to kill us, live among us? Is that how you will prove the alliance is solid? Why not let them stay and send Inga back?"

"You sound like a petulant child."

"I sound like a man who knows better than to trust the woman being forced upon me. You want this alliance for the sake of our clan. Right now. But what about when you are gone? What about when Mother is no longer the frú? You cannot deny the duties Mother shoulders, especially when you are away. Do you honestly see Inga able to do what Mother does? Do you honestly see Inga being able to lead and protect our people? You may get your alliance now to protect the tribe, but what are does destiny hold for us once you are gone?" Ivar leaned back in his chair and stared out at the sleeping members of his tribe.

"She will mature into the woman she needs to be," Soren sounded doubtful for the first time.

"There is maturity, but there is character. Inga doesn't have the character to be our frú. She doesn't have it to be anyone's frú. Inga is too selfish to put anyone's needs ahead of hers, let alone an entire homestead."

"You should have more faith in the woman you will live with for the rest of your life."

"Father," Ivar took a deep breath before broaching a topic everyone studiously avoided. "It's no secret that you and Mother do not get along. You never have, from what I've heard. But that's not the same as what you're sentencing me to. You and Mother may wish you hadn't married one another, but you trust and rely upon Mother. You *can* trust and rely upon her. Do you believe I can do that with Inga? Do you expect our people to do the same? You have set us all up for failure. There is no way she will be what Mother is, and our people will notice before the first moon is over. You and Mother are healthy and strong. You will both live many more years, but that will only give our people more years to dread Inga becoming their frú."

"You don't give her enough credit. She can grow to be what your Mother is."

"Did Mother have to grow to be what my amma was? Or did she arrive here already prepared to be your helpmate, to serve our people?"

Soren was trapped, and he realized it. He may have a miserable marriage, but he respected his wife. He did not like her, but he had to admit that much of it was not her fault. Soren had been in Ivar's position, forced to give up the woman he wanted for the sake of his people. But Soren had not fought for the woman he wanted. He had given in and let the woman go, not out of duty, but because he assumed one woman was as good as another. Soren's father had blessed him with a woman who ruled their homestead as well as his mother did, and Disa did well when Soren was away. But he had refused to accept Disa because she was not the woman he wanted. Soren bedded his wife and enjoyed the time with her; intimacy was the only thing upon which they agreed. His rejection and scorn damaged his marriage, however, before it had a chance to begin. He recognized that he had made his wife a bitter woman well before her time, but he was too prideful to admit to it and ask forgiveness.

Soren was aware Ivar was not exaggerating. He had seen Inga's propensity to narcissism during the young woman's visits. He had niggling doubts about her suitability, but he had pursued the alliance before he met her. Soren needed the feud to end before it impoverished and weakened the clan. Soren had observed how well Ivar got along with Thor's sons, particularly Rangvald, who he suspected would one day be jarl. Harold was too reckless, impetuous, and vain to not die young in battle. Soren had lost his own younger brother, Skarde, who shared a similar personality to Harold.

He allowed himself to consider Lena for the first time. He had known the woman since she was a baby. Her father had been one of his most trusted warriors until his injury kept him from fighting beyond simple home defense. Lena's mother had been close friends with Disa, welcoming her when his wife first arrived. Lena, Vigo, Eindride, and Ivar had gravitated towards one another as children. Even when other girls were beginning to train to be shieldmaidens, Lena invariably wound up training with Vigo, Eindride, and Ivar. As the three boys grew into young men, and their strength increased, Soren had assumed Lena would move on to spar and train with women. He could not have been more mistaken, nor could he have underestimated her more. Lena had an intuition for battle, and where she could not overpower his son, Vigo, and Eindride, she made a habit of outwitting them. She used her smaller frame and shorter sword to allow her to get closer to her opponent. Her blade landed across ribs, poking breast bones more times than not. While most of the men were stronger than her, she was by no means weak. She was the strongest and fastest of all his shieldmaidens. Unusually strong by most standards.

Soren also had to admit that where most of his shieldmaidens refused to consider household duties beyond what was necessary for them to run their homes, Lena excelled in that domain, too. She lost her mother when she was a young girl, but her grandmother stepped in to train her how to be a woman who managed a household and defend it while the men were away. Lena found a loving relationship with Disa, the daughter his wife never had. Lena worked alongside Disa for years, and Soren knew that inevitably, Lena learned what was needed to be a jarl's helpmate and a leader among the clan. There was little that Lena was unwilling to do, often taking on chores that even thralls despised because she was strong and understood someone needed to do the task regardless of its lack of appeal.

Soren had also seen how happy Lena made his son. It was a greater happiness than he had experienced, even with the woman he had wanted. A woman who had moved on and married another man within a moon of Soren's own marriage. Part of his resentment toward Disa came from his hurt that the woman he loved moved on so quickly and so happily. Soren still remembered the loving relationship his parents had developed, and he knew their love had made them better leaders. He and Disa had to work twice as hard to grow into such leaders because of their own hostility to one another.

For the first time in his life, Soren regretted his choices rather than resenting choices made for him. While he might be responsible for an entire homestead of people, he loved each of his children, and Ivar was the only one he had left. He did not want to sentence him to misery.

"Father?" Ivar tilted his head. "You've been silent an awfully long time."

Soren gazed at Ivar through a new set of eyes. He nodded as he leaned forward in his chair, one arm resting on the table as he twisted to face Ivar.

"You've given me a great deal to think about. More than I wanted to, but many things I should have considered years ago." Soren glanced around the gathering hall, a room where he had spent countless hours over the course of his life. He had fond and sad memories, and he had bitter ones from events that took place in that very space. When he looked back at Ivar, it shocked the son to see how the father seemed to age in a matter of a glance.

"I know you despise me, especially for the way I treat your mother, but I do love you and want the best for you. I have made a great many mistakes with your mother, but what you said about her is true. I can admit that," Soren said. "Your mother has been an admirable helpmate, and I couldn't ask for a better frú for our clan. I should have been a better husband. Perhaps if I had been, we wouldn't make each other so miserable."

It stunned Ivar how candid his father was being. They had never had such a conversation. Ivar did not think his father had ever spoken to anyone so openly. Not even his second-in-command, Eindride's father Magnus.

"I don't want Inga to sentence you to a life like I did your mother. I've refused to acknowledge Lena as a suitable wife for you because she has no connections to another clan. She cannot strengthen our position in the Trondelag through bloodlines, but I've failed to accept that she can strengthen our position by being a force to be reckoned with in her own right." Soren leaned in closer. "To be honest, if I were a jarl stupid enough to raid us, I would fear finding Lena defending the homestead more than anyone else. She is a bloodthirsty little thing."

Ivar could not believe what his father was saying. Ivar's heart raced as he listened to his father praise Lena for the first time since Soren had begun the marriage negotiations. He only nodded, too fearful that anything he said might alter the course of the conversation. He prayed the course was his father admitting Ivar should marry Lena.

"Ivar, we have signed the agreement, and the marriage will take place. I understand that is not what you want, and I realize now that it was a wrong decision, but we cannot back out. You were wise to insist this be a trial marriage. That said, you must give Inga a fair chance to become a wife you might keep. You cannot shortchange her the opportunity to prove herself. She may very well surprise you. If that's the case, you can keep Lena but acknowledge Inga as your wife."

Ivar's heart cringed, and he was shaking his head before he was aware what he was doing.

"I would never '*keep Lena*,' and she would never agree to be my mistress once I'm married. Inga would never accept it either. She would sooner see Lena dead than live with the competition or the slight." Ivar held up his hand before his father spoke.

"Nor am I marrying both of them. I have no desire to have two wives. Not when I don't even want the one I'm supposed to have. I will give Inga the chance you demand, but she will not be my wife in all senses. I refuse to bend on that."

Soren's mouth pursed in a scowl.

"You must bed her. You just agreed to give her a chance to prove herself as your wife. And that is one duty of being your wife. I will watch you the first time if I must."

"Father," Ivar did not hide the exasperation from his voice. "This takes us back to where we began. She is already bedding half the guards she brought with her. If I bed her, even if it's only the once, you can guarantee she will somehow fall pregnant, forcing me to keep her. She is manipulative and self-serving. Inga wants the title of frú, believes she's entitled to it, but she doesn't want any other part that goes along with it. She will claim a babe is mine to ensure she gets what she wants. Do you want to risk a child not of your blood becoming the next generation's heir?"

"Wear a sheath. Even if it's only the once tonight. Be sure she doesn't notice. Keep the candles out and the fire low. If she falls pregnant, then we will be onto her deception."

"She is an experienced woman. She will recognize the difference." Ivar warned.

"Distract her."

"Father--"

"Son," Soren's voice held a note of warning, and Ivar knew the time for candidness had ended.

Ivar nodded, but he would not go through with it. He was sure his father suspected that, so he was certain there would be at least one witness tonight.

. . .

The rest of the day dragged on for Ivar. While the minutes seemed to stretch on interminably, the hours suddenly flew by once evening approached and the death knell rang for Ivar. He slipped away on his horse with Vigo and Eindride riding beside him. They told Einar that they were going hunting and that Ivar wanted to bring back an offering for the feast. In truth, Ivar, Eindride, and Vigo wanted to waste enough time that there would be no chance for Ivar to go through the sword ritual. Ivar insisted—and his friends agreed—that he should save the ritual of searching within the burial catacombs for an ancestor's sword, marking the time when a boy transitioned into a man on the day of his wedding, for when Ivar married Lena. He treated that even as an inevitable part of his future rather than a possibility slipping through his fingers.

The three men arrived back with a boar and only enough time to bathe. Thor's scowl matched Soren's fierce frown, but there was nothing to be done short of delaying the ceremony. Ivar wanted to see Lena once more, to promise her one last time that he would sort this debacle out, but that would only endanger Lena. Between Inga's ire and the clan's gossip, it would leave Lena in an even more tenuous position. He prayed that Eindride would speak to Brenna before the end of the night's feast. He and Lena were depending upon the plan that Eindride would step in and replace him in Lena's life, or at least appear to replace him.

Eindride walked beside Ivar, nudging him when Ivar seemed to drag his feet as they walked to the altar that stood among the tall fir trees. Ivar scanned the crowd, searching for the flaxen braid that he had untangled the night before. He searched for the cobalt-blue eyes he had stared into for as long as he could remember. A memory flashed through his mind of when they were children. He had once compared Lena's eyes to the blue that sparked in a fire when dung was burned. He almost chuckled aloud when he remembered the blackened eye he received for the comparison.

Ivar found the face he looked for at the edge of the crowd. Lena stood with Tormud and Jan, but she looked small and alone to Ivar. He wanted to race to her, comfort her, but his feet continued to carry him to the altar. Only moments later he found Inga standing beside him. When he turned to face Inga, his eyes darted to the crowd, and he caught sight of the back of Lena's head as she slipped away. For the first time, Ivar allowed the fact that their relationship was over to take hold. He was aware that his mouth moved as he spoke the vows, but he could not tell a soul what he had said. He could not describe what Inga wore or what she said. There was nothing from the blessing that he could recall once it was over. The clan and Thor's entourage moved to the gathering hall where the feast started.

Lena was a glutton for punishment. She considered skipping the blessing ceremony, the idea of watching Ivar marry another woman was abhorrent, but she could not stay away. She had to see it for herself. However, the moment she realized Ivar was looking for her in the crowd, she could not bring herself to stay. Lena could not watch her future being handed over to another woman. She slipped away, certain Ivar had seen her, but unable to keep her composure any longer. She ran through the trees until she came to the edge of the longhouses. Lena rushed towards her own home even though there was no longer anyone around to witness her falling apart. Lena was nearly at her door when she sensed, more than saw or heard, someone approach. She drew the knife from her belt as she kept a steady pace in an attempt to fool her pursuer into believing she was unaware that he or she followed her.

Lena pushed through the door to her family's longhouse and slammed it shut only a moment before a thud made the wood rattle against her ribs. She dropped the bar into the slats, locking out whoever attempted to catch her. She ran across the main room just in time to bar the second door as the handle jangled and another thud came, but this time it sounded like an ax rather than a person. The woodpile stood just beside the kitchen door. Whoever was trying to gain entry now had a far more efficient tool than their body or a sword. She ran to her chamber and slipped on a pair of leather pants before yanking the over-tunic of her dress over her head. As the tunic slipped free of one arm, she was already reaching for her sword belt. Lena strapped it to her waist before adding two more knives to her belt. She touched the knives in each of her boots. She picked up the knife she carried into the longhouse but tossed on the bed as she changed. Lena put her ear to her chamber door and listened before opening it a crack. She heard an ax thunking against the door as someone attempted to hack their way into her home. Lena snatched her bow and quiver from where they rested near her door and slipped into her brother Jan's chamber. From her brother's chamber, she had a better line of sight to either of the doors leading outside. She nocked an arrow and waited.

Lena forced herself to breathe, calming her racing heart. Inevitably, someone would breach the door and enter her home. It was also inevitable that whoever dared would receive an arrow in the chest.

Even while she's getting married, that bitch can threaten me.

Lena suspected who arranged the impending attack. While Jarl Soren may have wanted Ivar to end things with her, he would not condone an attack on her, if not for Ivar's sake, then for the practical reason that she was one of his best warriors.

The door burst open, and Lena paused for only a heartbeat, ensuring it was a true enemy before she released the first arrow. It landed in a man's neck before he stumbled toward her. The next arrow went into the second man's chest. He was dead before he fell to the floor. Lena was ready to fire again when she recognized the beautiful fair skin and blonde hair that only belonged to Lorna. Her friend was winded and carrying a bloodied knife. As the man in front of Lorna fell, Lena realized that her arrow entered him from the front while Lorna's knife entered him from the back. Rangvald was close on Lorna's heels.

"We have to go," Rangvald's gaze swept across the main room of Lena's home. "Now."

Lorna stepped over the two dead men and met Lena halfway. Lorna pulled Lena into a tight embrace.

"We don't have time for that. We need to leave before more arrive."

"Och haud yer wheest, ye horrid mon. There is a moment to spare for a hug. The other three are already dead." Lorna tossed over her shoulder as she brushed Lena's hair from her face and looked her friend over. "No worse for wear. Gather some belongings, and we'll be off."

Lena looked at the dead men and nodded once before pivoting on her heel and going back to her chamber. No one spoke as Lena prepared to run from the only home she had ever known, and Lorna and Rangvald removed the bodies. As Lena followed her friends outside, she paused for a moment. Guilt filled her knowing she would leave bloodstains on the floor. She was certain her father and brother would panic.

"Don't worry. Brenna is the one who alerted us that you left and were being followed. She'll explain to Tormud and Jan, and she'll make sure Eindride follows close behind." Rangvald spoke over his shoulder as they crept toward the village stables. Sven greeted them with three saddled horses.

"I'm sorry on behalf of my family, Lena. We—" Sven raised his hands and shrugged, unable to come up with anything else to say.

"I know, Sven. You and your brothers, and Signy too, are nothing like Inga. It amazes me that it's possible that she and Signy pass as twins but are as different as rock and rain." Lena offered him a sad smile as Sven handed over the reins.

Rangvald, Lorna, and Lena rode out from the homestead, the sounds of the feast left in their wake.

THIRTEEN

Ivar considered drowning his sorrows in ale and mead, hoping he could get so drunk that no one would expect him to perform husbandly duties. But each sip of alcohol soured in his stomach and made him want to heave. Seated beside Inga, people made toasts not truly to congratulate the couple but as excuses for Ivar's clansmen and women to feast in excess. He wondered if any of them drank to console themselves, knowing what a miserable life they would one day have when he and Inga ruled the tribe.

"Drink up, husband," Inga purred beside his ear. "Drink and be merry."

Ivar dipped his chin but refused to even glance at Inga. She had been solicitous to the point of absurdity, and Ivar had only expended the minimum amount of courtesy expected of him. He oversaw the serving of Inga's meal and her first cup of ale. After that, he turned his attention to Eindride, but his friend had slipped away. He tried to spot Eindride and Brenna, for whom he suspected his friend abandoned him, but he could not see them either.

First Lena walked away. Now I can't see Eindride anywhere. Neither person who I need most is near to support me.

Neither of them can bear to see this sham. Where's Vigo? He's not here either.

"Husband," Inga's hand glided along the inside of his thigh, making its way higher until Ivar seized her wrist. The frailty of her bones made him careful not to hurt her, but it reminded him of how different she was from Lena. Lena's wrists were narrow too, but he never felt as if she might break. "I believe they will expect us to retire soon. I confess to needing some quiet."

"By all means, retire now. No one will disturb you." Ivar tried not to snarl, but Inga's gasp told him he failed.

"No one will disturb *us*," Inga hissed. "You will retire with me."

Inga's demand caught Ivar's attention. He squeezed her wrist mercilessly before tossing it away from him.

"Unless you would like to learn whether your brother's warning was true, I suggest you never, ever dictate to me what I will do or where I will go. Or what I won't do or won't go either."

"How dare you?"

"I dare because I can. Remember, I am your husband now. You belong to me to do with as I choose. And remember, I may send you back." Ivar pushed away from the table and swept his mug into his hand before losing himself in the crowd.

"Son, it is time. You can't avoid it any longer."

Ivar turned to find his mother standing just behind him. Her sympathetic smile and the sadness around her eyes tempted Ivar to collapse into her arms as he had when he was a child, but at the same time, it made him want to run far, far away. His mother was aware of the mistake that had been made. Ivar would even venture that his mother tried to intercede on his behalf. But that would have only made his father more emphatic to see the betrothal through. Now they expected him to bed the woman who insisted on marrying a man who did not want her. She wanted the position and the power more than she wanted the man. More than she cared if Ivar wanted her.

"She's gone to your chamber already," Disa offered when Ivar looked towards the head table. Signy, Ulfhild and Inga have gone to prepare Inga for your wedding night.

Ivar's mouth went dry, and he took an unconscious step back. He looked about wildly, hoping against hope that an excuse to flee would materialize; alas, there was no reason for him to remain. He noticed that many people were looking at him with sly grins, and a few bawdy comments floated on the air. The people gathered for the feast now expected him to feast on his bride. He nodded at Disa and turned away. He made his way through the crowd as people clapped him on the back and tossed suggestions for how to pleasure his young bride. It tempted him to tell them that his bride was more likely to teach him than the other way around.

He paused when he came to the door of his chamber. He listened for a moment but could not make out any of the words coming from the space he had only shared with Lena. Ivar knocked once and pushed the door open, but before he closed it, his father followed him in, along with his mother. Ivar wanted to groan, knowing there would be an audience.

Ivar nodded to his new mother-in-law and sister-in-law. The very notion that he had more family because he spoke words he could not even remember seemed ridiculous. He counted among his few blessings that Inga's parents drew the line at her father and brothers being present for the bedding.

"Hello, my love," Inga whispered as she stepped before Ivar. She ran her hands over his chest, and Ivar attempted to hide his revulsion at both her words and her touch. When Inga lifted onto her toes to kiss Ivar, he stepped away. Ivar walked to the fire and used the poker to push apart the logs, causing the blazing flames to splutter and dim. He moved to each of the candles and blew them out.

"I thought it might be easier for you. Less embarrassing for my young bride." Ivar's words were a soft-spoken taunt, a dare to see if Inga would admit to her experience. Inga nodded once, but her seductive smile slid, and a cold look of calculation took its place. She stepped toward Ivar once more, this time pressing her body against his as she looked up expectantly.

"I am your eager student, my love." Inga purred, but the sound grated against Ivar's nerves as much as her words. Everyone present knew there was no love between them. She wound her hand through his hair and pressed none too gently until Ivar bent his head. It was Inga who initiated the kiss, but Ivar did not pull away. He rested his hands on her waist and tried to clear his mind as Inga's and Lena's faces danced before his closed eyes, Ivar forced himself to relax as he tried to persuade himself that kissing Inga did not make him unfaithful to Lena, that she would understand the situation. Ivar knew Lena did, but it did not make his guilt any less suffocating.

Perhaps if I pretend that it is Lena I'm kissing then I can go through with this. Ivar conjured a picture in his mind from the summer when he took Lena on a picnic near the shoreline. Ivar and Lena had stripped and raced each other into the water, swimming and making love before emerging to lay naked on the sandy shore. They had fed each other, spending more time kissing than eating. They eventually abandoned their meal in exchange for devouring one another. Ivar remembered how erotic it had been to watch pleasure sweep Lena away with pleasure as his tongue worked her pearl. *Yes. This might work. If I imagine it's Lena instead, then maybe I can get through this. I cannot escape now. Not with my parents and her family here. Thank gods I put the sheath on the last time I slipped outside to relieve myself.*

However, there was an obstacle Ivar seemed unable to overcome. While his mind was willing to imagine it was Lena he was kissing, his body refused to do the same. His body did not stir at all as Inga's hands roamed over him. When her hand slid to his rod, her gasp was from the shock of finding nothing hard rather than from finding something intimidating. Ivar smothered it by thrusting his tongue into her mouth, but he gagged at the sour taste that met him. His hands attempted to distract him, but Inga's body was so different from Lena's. Her hips were broader and her backside more generous, but not in a way that aroused him. Her lack of physical activity showed in her physique, and it only reminded him that she was spoiled and unaccustomed to hard work. His mind flooded with images of Lena training and working alongside his mother, both backbreaking work at times. As his other hand slid up to her breast, the flesh was not supple and round like Lena's. Instead, they felt deflated and small compared to Lena's. While Lena had a lithe form, she was well endowed. Once again, the differences between the woman he wanted and the woman he stood before filled his mind and made his head ache.

Ivar flinched when Inga's nails trailed a little too sharply along his abdomen. She slid her hands beneath Ivar's tunic while he was unaware. She tweaked his nipple painfully and bit his lip when he jerked way. The look she cast him was her own dare. She challenged him to see if he would complain, but when he did little to react, she cocked an eyebrow before whipping her chemise over her head. Ivar looked at Inga and found nothing about her stirred him.

"Come now, husband," Inga chuckled at her own double entendre, but Ivar found little humor in Inga's words or actions. If anyone had wondered if she was a virgin, her haste to undress would have eased their curiosity. She pushed the hem of his tunic as high as she could reach before Ivar was forced to pull it over his head and shoulders. Inga grasped it from him and flung it away. She reached for the laces of his leather pants, but Ivar was not ready for more than one reason. His body still refused to respond to her enticement, and he did not want her to see how flaccid he remained or that he had a sheath on. He inched her backwards until her legs hit the bed.

"On," he growled.

Inga giggled, thinking Ivar was coming around to the notion of bed sport. She climbed onto the bed, presenting her backside to him. She looked over her shoulder and wiggled her hips in invitation. Ivar attempted not to grimace as he looked at a body that was not Lena's. Guilt once more had a stranglehold. He might try to rationalize and justify coupling with Inga, but he knew it would never be right. And even if Lena understood the situation, it would not eliminate the hurt and sense of betrayal it would cause.

A deep clearing of a throat brought Ivar's attention back to the woman on his bed. His father's presence only made the entire scene worse. Ivar had been trying to ignore the onlookers, but his father's reminder that he needed to bed Inga made ignoring them impossible. He climbed onto the bed and between Inga's thighs. He rested his weight on one forearm as he rubbed his own hand over his soft cock. Ivar closed his eyes, and as he had countless times over the years when it was impossible to be with Lena, he imagined it was her hand instead of his. His body began to respond, and when he was semi-aroused, he turned his attention back to Inga. He kept a picture of Lena in his mind as he squeezed his eyes shut. He kissed along Inga's neck toward her breasts as he pushed the opening of his pants over his hardening length. When his mouth reached her nipple, he flicked out his tongue before suckling. Her breast was not wholly unsatisfying, so with an image of Lena still floating before his eyes, he moved to the other breast. Ivar continued to stroke himself, but shifted away when Inga attempted to reach for him. He could not afford for her to discover the sheath that covered his cock. He kissed his way down her belly until he settled between her thighs. She hooked her knees over his shoulders as she lifted her hips in offering. Ivar's nose crinkled when he caught a particularly strong whiff of the oil that someone had rubbed into Inga's skin. It was not the blend of lavender and incense that Lena favored, the latter fragrance a new addition since their voyage to the Mediterranean. Instead it was some sickly-sweet scent that he did not recognize and did not like. Bile rose in the back of his throat as he considered what he had been about to do. Such an intimacy made his throat burn. Now that it had distracted him, it was impossible to fool himself into imagining it was Lena he was about to make love to. He shifted back to rest his forearms near Inga's shoulders.

The soft moans and mewls that Inga made were grating on Ivar's nerves as they grew louder. The falseness of them made him want to slap her. She was not any more aroused than he was. The noises were for show, and they irritated him. Ivar looked into Inga's cold eyes and a wave of nausea rose from his gut. Nothing about Inga was right. She did not look right, she did not taste right, she did not smell right, she did not sound right, and she most definitely did not feel right. She was not Lena.

"Come now," Inga repeated her earlier suggestion as she reached for Ivar, her hand covering his which was once again stroking his cock. She guided his hand and his rod to her entrance and raised her hips. The moment the tip of Ivar's sword slid against Inga's sheath, he was certain he would be ill. He leaped from the bed and dashed to the chamber pot where he heaved until his entire evening meal revisited him. He wiped his mouth along the back of his hand before turning to his parents. His revulsion towards Inga and the situation transferred to his father and mother. He shook his head as he stepped past them, righting his pants with each step until he stood beside his shirt. He swept it from the floor before glaring at his father.

"You want this that badly, you fuck her." Ivar pulled the door open so hard that it slammed against the wall before slamming shut with him on the other side.

Once outside, Ivar did not think about where he was going. There was only one destination. He would fall on his knees before Lena and beg her forgiveness while praying he never had to reveal just how close he had come to coupling with another woman, never had to admit that his hands and mouth had touched another woman. Ivar had not realized he was sweating until an icy blast of air hit his damp skin. He shivered as he pulled his tunic back on then ran to Lena's home.

Before Ivar entered, he sensed something was wrong. There were several dents in the wood where it looks as if someone had used the hilt of a sword to bang against it. Ivar knocked but did not wait for anyone to answer. He stepped inside and found Tormud and Jan standing with Einar. All three were staring at something on the floor. As Ivar approached, he recognized the stain was blood.

"Lena? Where is she? What happened?" Ivar ran to Lena's chamber door and pushed it open, but there was no one there. He noticed that her sword belt and her bow and quiver not in their usual place. He spun around and glared at Tormud. "She left."

It was a statement, an accusation rather than a question. Tormud nodded as Jan motioned for Ivar to follow him. The young man who was much like a younger brother to Ivar, especially after he lost his own, paused before opening the kitchen door.

"We aren't sure what happened. We only arrived home a few minutes ago, then Einar showed up," Jan whispered before letting Ivar pass through the door.

Ivar took in the five dead bodies, two with arrows through them. One glance told him that Lena had shot the two men, since the fletching was her distinct pattern or feathers.

"Where is she?" Ivar croaked before clearing his voice.

"We don't know," Jan pushed the door closed, leaving Tormud and Einar inside. "Einar said that Brenna came running to tell Eindride that he had to leave. That everything was happening now. When Eindride gave Brenna a quick kiss and bolted out of the gathering hall, Einar followed him to the stables. Apparently, Rangvald and Lorna caught three men before they reached here. Two of the men followed Lena and broke through the door."

Jan turned and ran his hand over the splintered wood. Ivar watched Jan set his shoulders and his chest broadened as his chin came up.

"These men tried to attack my sister. They should thank Odin that it was Rangvald and Lorna who happened upon them. I would have chopped off their bollocks and made them eat it before allowing anyone to kill them." Jan spat on the bodies before releasing a string of oaths Ivar had not realized Jan knew. "Eindride followed Rangvald, Lorna, and Lena's trail to the south. Einar came to tell us."

Ivar shook his head as he backed away from Jan. He turned just in time to cast up his accounts on the grass rather than Jan's feet. When he stormed out of his chamber, he had been sure there was nothing left in his belly, but fear and anger fused together and forced the last of his dinner from him. Ivar pulled the door open and stepped back into the longhouse.

"Ivar, what are you doing here?" Tormud asked.

"I couldn't do it. I won't. I came to see Lena."

"On your wedding night," Einar sounded perplexed, but there was an edge to his tone that caught Ivar's attention. He nodded as he watched the boy who was turning into a man. Ivar realized that neither Jan nor Einar were boys anymore. He sensed Jan was chomping on the bit to go with him when he chased after Lena. He wondered if Einar would ask to join them.

"It was not a real wedding. Everyone knows that. Since this isn't a real marriage, there was no need for a wedding night." Ivar watched Einar's reaction and was certain he saw a spark of hatred before it vanished.

"I know where my brother was going to meet the others," Einar offered.

"They are on their way to Kaupang. I already know." Ivar looked over at Jan. "Gather what you need and meet me at the stables."

"Are you bringing her back?" Tormud asked.

"No. Not until I'm convinced there's no threat. I

will ensure she's safe, but I won't bring her back yet." No one needed to say aloud who or what the threat was.

Einar watched Ivar pace as Jan gathered the few items he would travel with. He clenched his jaw and his fists, wanting to plow the latter into Ivar's jaw. Einar was aware that Inga planned the attack; after all, he was the one who paid the guardsmen. However, Ivar was supposed to bedding Inga, so Einar could be the one who chased after them. Einar was supposed to reach Lena and the others before Ivar could. Einar was going to convince them that Ivar wanted Lena to return. He was going to show Lena that he was her protector when men attacked them on the road. He would show his fealty to Ivar when he chose Lena over the others, so no one blamed him if Rangvald, Lorna, and even his own brother Eindride died. Now the plan seemed to fizzle as his temper flared. He sucked in deep breaths through his nostrils, trying to control the anger threatening to overwhelm him.

"I can show you the route Eindride took," Einar offered again. He wanted to drive his knife into Ivar's back when the man did not even bother to face Einar but tossed his response over his shoulder.

"I know which way. You're needed here."

Einar waited to see if Ivar would elaborate about how he was needed, but Einar realized Ivar was just placating him. Tormud would be the one who informed the jarls and frús about Ivar's absence. He wondered if there would be a way to keep Tormud from going to Soren before he spun the story to his advantage. Einar considered the ax that rested once more beside the door. His pulse thumped in his ears as his heart raced. If he did away with Tormud, that would be one less barrier to being with Lena. He would be the shoulder she turned to in her grief while Inga kept Ivar occupied.

Einar coupled with Inga just that morning, and he intended to join with her several more times that night now that he would not be accompanying Ivar. He would set the other part of his plan in motion; he would get Inga with child, his child, as quickly as the goddess Freyja allowed. Lena would never try to draw Ivar away from his wife and child. Einar would once again be there to console her. He glanced once more at the ax and inched toward the door.

"Einar, you'd better come with me. We need to let Jarl Soren and Jarl Thor know what is happening." Tormud eyed the young man who was a similar age to his own son. Einar struck him as younger than Jan with a spoiled and temperamental nature, yet there was something that made Einar's mind work in a way reserved for an experienced warrior. The young man had a gleam in his eye like a berserker who smelled blood. Tormud did not miss Einar's momentary flinch as though he would rebel against Tormud's suggestion that they go together. Tormud would keep an eye on him and never walk in front of the man.

In less than a quarter of an hour, Jan had packed and both he and Ivar were mounted, charging toward the gate to the homestead.

"Ivar!"

Ivar twisted to see his father racing after him. Sword drawn. Ivar reined in, but he refused allow anyone to delay him.

"Where do you think you are going? Are you fleeing like a coward?" Soren spat the accusation at his son as he pointed the tip of his sword at Ivar's chest. Ivar's nostrils flared as he batted the sword away and leaned toward his father.

"The only coward is you. You are too fearful to admit you've made an error in welcoming Inga into this tribe. Now she's had Lena attacked. Lena's fled with Eindride, Rangvald, and Lorna. The bitch's own brother would rather rescue my woman than stand beside his sister."

"You lie," Soren spluttered. "You just hoped to run away from your duties so you can rut with your whore."

Ivar whipped his horse around but looked back at his father. The look of hatred made Soren take a step back.

"I will *never* forgive you for that comment. If you weren't my father, I'd kill you for calling Lena that. Call her that again, and I will." Ivar spurred his forward. "Check the bodies outside Lena's home. They're Thor's men. Why would they be there?"

Ivar and Jan galloped through the gates and onto the road that would take them south and to Lena and their friends. Soren looked around and found Tormud and Einar standing together. He caught an expression on Einar's face that he was not sure how to interpret, but it was gone in an instant. He walked to Tormud's side as he sheathed his sword.

"You were once a great warrior to me. Your wife was my wife's best friend. You have never asked for anything, not even when your daughter became my son's companion. Tell me true."

Tormud looked into Soren's eyes, and the jarl sensed he would not like the story they would tell him.

"Lena couldn't watch the blessing, so she went home. Men must have followed her because there was blood on the floor in the main room of my longhouse, but Lena was not there. I couldn't find her sword or bow and arrows, and the dress she wore was tossed onto the bed. She always hangs up her clothing. The ax by my woodpile is bloody, and there are five dead guardsmen from Jarl Thor's tribe. They splintered the door from my kitchen by hacking it open, and there are dents in the front door."

Soren drag his hand over his face before rubbing it across his nape. He turned to look at his longhouse where his new ally seethed at the disgrace Ivar caused by shunning Inga. He glanced back at Tormud, then at Einar, who was staring at the jarl's longhouse. Once again, he saw something in the young man's face that made him uneasy. It was almost a look of glee that there was trouble brewing. Soren caught Tormud's eye before lifting his chin toward Einar then tilted his head away. Tormud stepped with Soren as both men watched their departure go unnoticed by Einar. Or at least they thought until Einar grinned at them, dipped his head, then dashed toward his home.

"He needs watching. He knows mores that he's telling." Tormud muttered.

"What makes you think that?"

"The same things that make you think it too. He was angry that Ivar chose Jan to travel with him. His gaze shifted between me and my ax one too many times to make me comfortable. It's as though he expects something more will happen, as though he's planning for something else. When Ivar refused him, I believe it shifted his plan enough to consider murdering me."

"Murder? Don't you think that's farfetched?"

"How many battles did I go into on your behalf? On your father's? I came home from them all. I even survived the last one that nearly took my leg. It wasn't by chance. I'm familiar with what a man looks like when he intends to kill you. Soren, I'm neither feeble-bodied nor feeble-minded, so don't speak to me as such." It was Tormud's longtime friendship and service to Soren that allowed him to speak so brazenly. "In the meantime, you haven't asked whether I think they injured Lena or if I think she'll be safe. You might remember you will be short two of your best warriors if your son's bride kills her. If that happens, neither Lena nor Ivar will return. Ivar will never forgive you, and I'm not sure that the rest of the tribe would either."

"She is but one shieldmaiden." Soren frowned with disbelief.

"She is the shieldmaiden that all the other women follow. Lena is the shieldmaiden that every man trusts to fight alongside him. She is the woman the thralls gladly work for. She has been the voice of reason and strategy to Ivar before every battle since they first clashed swords as children. Lena is the woman this tribe wishes would one day help Ivar lead. No one here thinks your alliance is worth the peace lost within our own homes now that Inga is to remain." Tormud shook his head as he looked at his friend from childhood. He and Eindride and Einar's father had grown up with Soren and trained together before sailing together to foreign lands. He knew Soren better than most.

"You are blind to not see Rangvald will one day lead Thor's tribe. Harold will get himself killed with his pride and recklessness. Rangvald and Ivar are much alike, and it's their respect for one another that will make them the greatest allies the Trondelag has ever seen. Their women will see to it. And I do not mean Inga. Bah, she will be nothing but *Ógæfa*, misfortune. She will be our downfall. It will Lena and Lorna. Soren, you're one of my oldest friends, but if any harm comes to my daughter, I will hold you responsible, just as Ivar will. You had better hope that Lena's *hemingja* is watching over her and continues to grant her good luck, or the blame will be on your shoulders."

Tormud limped toward his home, and he left Soren standing alone. He looked around his home, the village he had spent his life serving. Everyone was correct. Lena had always been the right choice, but now he was not sure that fate would smile upon them twice. His insistence on having his way may well have changed fate, and now they would have to weather the consequences of Soren believing he controlled the future. Soren caught movement as he walked toward his longhouse. A young man was running toward the back of his house. If he was not mistaken, it was Einar. The only chambers on that side of the building were for guests. Soren had a sinking feeling that he had already figured out where Einar was going.

FOURTEEN

"Hurry," Inga hissed as Einar scrambled through her window. Inga leaned out of the opening and looked around. When she was convinced no one had seen her late-night visitor, she pulled the fur covering over the window.

Einar pulled Inga against him and ravished her mouth with a brutal kiss that had Inga melting against him. He bit her lower lip as he spanked her backside, the sound ringing throughout the chamber.

"You don't issue orders to me," Einar hushed tones held menace that both frightened and titillated Inga.

"Yes, Einar. I'm sorry." Inga pulled her robe open. She lifted her breasts in offering to him, and he did not need a second invitation. He pinched and twisted one nipple as he suckled her other breast. Inga tried to swallow her moans as she clung to Einar's shoulder and fisted his hair. "Please don't make me wait. I've missed you so since this morning."

"Ivar not satisfy you? Not enough for you?" Einar sneered.

"He couldn't get it up. Then when he did, he couldn't go through with it. He vomited, then ran away like a little girl." Inga's scorn made Einar chuckle.

"Well, you had better get him hard and up to the task, or you will have a very hard time explaining how you're carrying his child."

"Are you--" Inga was breathless as she looked at the ridge hidden by Einar's leather pants.

"Am I going to take you again?" Einar whispered in her ear as he once again tweaked her nipple. "Yes. Everywhere. Down."

Einar pressed Inga's shoulder until she knelt before him. His head dropped back as she released his cock and lowered her mouth onto him. It was impossible to overlook that she knew what she was doing. Even if he had no one to compare her with, she made him want to climax with only a few passes of her tongue. When she ran her teeth along the ridge on the underside of his rod, he leaked. Einar let her continue to work him closer to release until he was close to losing control. He grasped her hair and pulled her to her feet before tearing the nightgown from her body. He pushed her toward a chair that sat before the fire. Einar bent her forward over the high back before bringing his hand down in a series of punishing spanks.

"You had but one duty tonight, Inga. You were to make Ivar bed you. You were to have him spill inside you. What if you're already with child? My child. How will you pass him off as Ivar's son if the man's never plowed your field?"

"I'm sorry, Einar. My mother and sister were there. Both of his parents, too. I think he couldn't perform with an audience."

"Ha," Einar's laugh was hollow. "He's barely gotten Lena out of sight before fucking her. There have been plenty of times when both he and Lena were aware everyone heard them, and it would have taken but a stretch of the neck to watch them. Ivar doesn't fear performing as a man in front of anyone. More likely he didn't want you."

Inga gasped; a ragged sob followed. Einar smiled at the back of Inga's head. He grasped her backside and nudged her feet apart. Einar pulled her hips toward him, letting his cock slide along her sheath, her dew coating him. He swept his fingers into her sheath then took the moisture and pressed against her most sacred spot. Einar fisted himself twice before thrusting into Inga, disregarding her cry of pain. It excited him.

"You know who wants you, don't you, my sweet Inga? I do. Feel how hard I am for you. Fell how tight your arse is around me. I won't last long." Einar thrust over and over as Inga gripped the arms of the chair. "But you like it like this, don't you?"

"Yes," Inga croaked. "I do. Only you understand."

"That's right. Only I understand what you need. Only I can give you it." Einar pulled her head back and captured her mouth, but where the first kiss was callous and possessive, this one was tender. The contradiction of how their bodies moved together and their mouths fused excited them both, but for different reasons. Feeling wanted at last combined with her physical need to be aroused made Inga willing to accept any of Einar's demands. The control he had over Inga and the pleasure her body gave him inflamed Einar.

"Can I?" Inga whispered, and Einar reveled in silence at the perverse pleasure of knowing that he already controlled Inga's mind and her body. It had taken but one day for her to accept that her body no longer climaxed without Einar's consent. Einar would have thought her need for approval pathetic if it did not give him physical satisfaction and dominance over her.

"Yes, my little one. You may climax."

On cue, Inga moaned as her core spasmed around him. Einar's body tried to follow Inga over the edge. He pulled free and thrust into her sheath long enough to spill before pulling out. He swept Inga into his arms and carried her to the bed. Einar was surprisingly gentle as he slid between the furs next to her. Her eyes were closed as she panted, her body still trembling. He caressed her belly and breasts before cupping her mons. He stroked her pearl until Inga shuddered again and curled into his body. Einar lifted her chin and once again kissed her. This time, he realized, he meant the tenderness. Something shifted in his chest as he watched how trusting she was. She looked young and vulnerable, which was what he had intended. Though he originally wanted the vulnerability purely to manipulate her, now it made him want to protect her and care for her. Einar grazed his hand over Inga's body until his palm rested against her backside. His thumb swept back and forth without his notice as he considered why his feelings for Inga shifted.

Einar still loved Lena. He wanted to possess her as much as he did Inga, but for very different reasons. He wanted to possess Lena for her unparalleled beauty. Einar wanted every man to know she chose him; he wanted the status she would bring him. He wanted Lena to depend upon him as he provided for her both emotionally and physically. As he looked down at the now-sleeping Inga, he wanted to possess her, and not only for the access her position afforded him. He wanted her because she understood his body's needs because they were hers too. She submitted to him in a way he never imagined Lena would. Inga gave herself to Einar without question or hesitation, wanting to please him. In turn, he found he wanted to please her, too. His heart softened as he held Inga. He would never stop wanting Lena; his obsession had driven him too long, but he found that having Inga made him happy in a way he had not considered.

Soren no longer heard what the couple said after Einar's first reprimand to Inga, but he did hear the unmistakable sounds of them coupling. He shook his head, knowing the rumors that even he had heard were true. Ivar had not needed to tell him that Inga was loose with her favors. He had overhead some of his men discussing how they had sampled her after the last visit. It tempted Soren to call off the negotiations. For better or for worse, Disa never would have disrespected him, herself, or their position within their tribe by bedding warriors he commanded. Inga seemed to not have those reservations. Now, she was coupling with a young man the same age as her. Soren understood what attracted them to one another, especially after Ivar's shameful rejection, but he could not allow Inga to cuckold Ivar. He would not risk having Einar's bastard inheriting his jarldom one day.

Soren turned and rested his back against the wall and shut his eyes for a moment as the sound of the couple finishing floated through the window. He shook his head and resolved the trial marriage had to end. Soren had already decided as much even before the ceremony, then Lena's disappearance confirmed it and Inga's infidelity necessitated it. He just had to figure out how. Soren made his way around to the entrance to the longhouse.

"Disa!" Soren called out.

Disa looked out from the kitchens and scowled.

Soren normally would have felt his temper spike, but his wife responded as she did after years of him belittling her. He recognized that she was waiting for his words to strike. He held out his hand and waited. Disa's head turned away as her brow flickered. She walked to him and looked down at his hand.

"Please. I need you," Soren whispered. He flinched as Disa's eyes took on a smug expression. He realized she assumed he meant he wanted to bed her, and he did after listening to Inga and Einar rutting, but that could wait. "I need to talk to you. I need your advice."

Disa's shock might have been amusing if it did not sting that admitting he needed her for something other than bed sport had such an effect on her. Soren remained silent until they entered their chamber. He bolted the door and dropped the bar. He led Disa to the fire and motioned for her to sit on the pillows before the hearth. Soren sank onto the fur next to her. As he watched the light from the flames flicker across her cheeks, her beauty struck him for the thousandth time, but the years had added lines and creases where they should not have yet been. He reached out a hand and ran his thumb along her cheek. Soren watched Disa's gaze shutter as she assumed he only wanted to couple.

"I did these to you," he whispered. "I caused these lines that should be here from laughing, not from tears and strain."

Soren watched Disa swallow, but otherwise she sat like a statue. He swept the pad of his thumb along the lines that bracketed her mouth. Ones that might appear as though there were from laughing, but he admitted they were from years spent frowning. He tucked strands of hair behind Disa's ear and noticed for the first time the gray hairs at her temples.

"Disa, I have failed you since before you even

arrived. I was a child in a man's body, and since I couldn't strike out at my father for taking away my favorite toy, I took it out on you. I thought you were root vegetables when I wanted my sweets back."

Disa spluttered, then chuckled. "You have called me many things, Sor, but root vegetables? That is too ridiculous to take offense at."

"Root vegetables are good for me. They strengthen me and make me better. Sweets don't last and aren't worth much past the first bite." Soren hoped his wife understood his horrible metaphor. When she stared at him, he thought he had offended her, but a gradual smile pulled at the corner of her mouth.

"Why are you doing this?"

"Because our son has taken me to task and forced me to grow up. I may lead this tribe and may have been a man since I swore my fealty to my father, but I never fully grew up. Or perhaps I never grew out of my selfishness. Disa, I understand an apology doesn't undo more than twenty years of disappointment and hurt, but I am sorry. I have been since early on, but not enough to swallow my pride. However, now that I see I'm sentencing Ivar to the life I sentenced you to, I wish I could go back. There is so much I would do differently, better."

"And I wish it was as simple as saying I forgive you. I don't know if I can." Disa admitted as she turned to look into the fire.

"Dee, one day we will be grandparents. Ivar had my parents as models of a good and happy marriage. He didn't have that with us. I would have his children see their parents and grandparents happy."

Disa shook her head and frowned. "Even if we can make amends, I cannot believe there will ever be happiness between Ivar and Inga."

"There never will be. She can't stay, Dee. We

have to send her back. You tried to warn me. I even saw the warning signs, but I was so certain I was making the right decision. That only *I* could make the right decision that I ignored everything that told me Inga is the wrong choice. Now I've seen it with my own eyes. Dee, she's rutting with Einar. From what I heard, it wasn't the first time either. She is already cuckolding Ivar, and they haven't even been wed a day."

Disa's eyes widened in shock, and she turned her head in the guest chambers' direction as if she saw Inga through walls and space.

"No matter how much effort and time you put into teaching her, I doubt there is any chance she will ever mature into the woman you are. I've made your life hard enough. You don't deserve that punishment. Not when there is already a woman who has proven repeatedly that she will one day run this household and village as well as you have since the day you arrived."

"Who?"

"You already know, as does everyone else, even I have despite refusing to admit it. Lena."

"Thank the gods you admitted it. But it's too late."

"No," Soren denied. "It can't be. We can't let it be. We will return the dowry when she leaves. We have to make it her choice, but Dee, she can't stay. A marriage between her and Ivar won't benefit anyone."

"Ivar, Harold, Rangvald, and Sven have become good friends over the past few months. I don't think the feud will last beyond you and Thor. Even if things devolve, and Thor takes insult, neither you nor he will live forever." Dee grinned at Soren's mock gasp. "You'll both move on to Valhalla or Fólkvangr, and it will be the boys who determine the next generation's wellbeing. It's better they are friends than merely neighbors who tolerate one another."

"Dee, I have always trusted you and known I can rely on you. I'm grateful for that. I just wish that I listened to you on this instead of being so disagreeable. You've given me steady and worthy advice over the years, and one of the few things I've gotten right is listening to you. But this time, I wanted to be right on my own. I wanted to be right the more I realized my error in considering this marriage. I should have listened to you."

"Are you admitting you were wrong? That even you make mistakes?" The teasing tone in her voice surprised Disa. There was something about seeing Soren humbled and almost vulnerable that eased the animosity she wore like armor.

"I am. Dee, there's something else you need to know." Soren's solemn gaze made Disa nervous. She feared what he might say. "I've never strayed from you. I'm certain Ivar and many others believes I have, but that must come from assuming you and I don't satisfy one another here in our chamber since we haven't gotten along anywhere else. I think some of our people even assumed I would approach Lorna when she was a guest, but I didn't. I saw one of my guardsmen approach her door a couple of nights when she first arrived, but I had no intention of going near it. I'm sure you've wondered, and I've given you reason to assume I have, but I haven't. And not merely because our coupling has always been satisfying. I didn't understand it until now, but I do. I never wanted another woman because no woman could live up to you. I think I've been bitter that you are such a good wife because I couldn't rationalize being unfaithful to a woman who does everything everyone expects and then more. I wanted to find fault with you, a real fault, not my perceived fault.

But being so disloyal to you after all you do for me as your husband and jarl, as well as for this tribe, seemed dishonorable to even consider."

"It was the same for me, Sor. I have wanted to hate you in truth, not just dislike you, but except for how we don't get along, I can't find real fault with you. You are a good leader and a good father. I may not have agreed with your decision about this marriage, but I understand you didn't make it lightly. You considered it because our tribe needs peace to prosper. Even before we met Inga, you regretted that Ivar would have to make such a sacrifice by marrying someone other than Lena. I know that wasn't easy for you, even if you haven't admitted that you worried about them."

"So, what do we do?"

"I don't know. But we will figure it out. For our people and for our son."

Soren and Disa looked at one another, and something shifted between them. There was the arousal that they always experienced, each of them attracted to the other even when they disliked each other. But this was different. It was not physical, or at least not entirely. The tension that seemed to have seeped into their very souls released.

"I don't want to fight anymore, Dee. We have spent what will have been the first half of our marriage baiting and lashing out at one another. We have a second half to make of what we want. I want to know that I will grow old with someone who wants to be at my side, not someone who is merely too old to get away."

Soren grinned, and Disa recognized the boyish playfulness that she witnessed when she first arrived more than two decades ago, but back then, it had not been directed at her. It had been toward another woman. It had broken her heart, and it was in that moment that she steeled herself against letting Soren ever break it again. Now it was directed at her, and she was unsure if she wanted to bask in its warmth or sob for the years of lost opportunity.

Soren watched the conflict and confusion shimmer in Disa's eyes, and he imagined he knew what caused it. He rarely smiled, and when he did, it was almost never a genuine smile directed at her. There had been disingenuous ones and mocking ones, but not a true one like he wore now. He inched closer to her and wrapped his arm around her waist.

"Perhaps we are in agreement to reconcile, but I don't expect you to overlook or forget the past. I just hope we can get to know one another as we want to be now, not as we have been or what we were. I have made you grow into a woman you never intended to. I remember when you used to smile and joke with my mother. You stopped laughing once both my parents were gone, and after the boys died, I don't think you've smiled since then. Not the way you used to when it reached your eyes and made them shine."

"You saw my eyes shine?"

"Yes. Of course." Soren tilted his head back. "You are so beautiful, Disa. I've never told you that when we aren't in the midst of joining. But you are. Your beauty has made me lust for you since I met you. I didn't want to. I blamed you for my own feelings. But your eyes shone when you arrived, but each year, they have dimmed until they seemed to burn out when the boys died. I did nothing to try to bring that light back. I made you suffer in silence in your grief instead of letting us console each other in our shared loss. I don't think you even considered for a moment turning to me. And that isn't what a marriage should be. You should be able to rely on me like I have relied on you. You have given, and I have taken."

"Sor, kiss me." Disa pulled her lips into a thin line, nervous to ask. "I want to see if it might be different now."

Soren cupped her cheek and inched closer, allowing Disa to start the kiss. It was as though they were kissing for the first time. They were both timid and unsure. Their lips brushed together several times before they both grew brave enough to press their mouths together. The kiss was languid as they explored one another. They had never struggled to be intimate, their mutual physical attraction and acceptance that they had no other choices for a lover made their coupling easy. Lust and need had sparked passion but not tenderness. Over the years, they came together for physical release and pleasure. Emotions other than lust had little to do with their coupling.

Now their kiss was filled with a sense of newness, as if they were younger versions of themselves. Soren kissed along Disa's cheek and jaw before moving to her neck, and she tilted her head, offering access to her neck. They drifted as they undressed one another before stretching out before the fire. Soren took time to observe Disa for the first time in years. Her belly had rounded over the years from carrying four sons. Her hips and backside were wider and softer, but he found he appreciated it, even if he never gave it much thought. He pressed her onto her back and swept her hair from beneath her shoulders. His fingers traced the fine lines that ran over her belly, the evidence of the family they created together. Soren shifted to kiss the scars before kissing each of her breasts.

"I've never thanked you for the sons you bore me. I believe there is little, or more likely nothing, you can't do." Soren suckled each breast as Disa arched toward his warm mouth.

"We made those sons together. You gave them to me as I gave them to you."

Soren ran his hand between Disa's thighs, and she let them fall open as they kissed. She burrowed her fingers into his hair as his fingers slipped into her. Her body reacted as it always did, humming with need and unspent passion. Disa grazed her nails over his chest and belly until she wrapped her hand around Soren's length. She remembered the first time she had touched him, intrigued and tentative. She had shut her eyes, so she did not have to look at a man she desired but did not like. Lying before the fire, she looked at a body she had admired countless times during more than twenty years of marriage. Her husband was a handsome man still in his prime.

"Sor, I desire you just as much now as I did all those years ago. Perhaps more. I will admit to always feeling superior to the other wives, knowing you were such a handsome man when we were young, and now when many of the men our age are growing slow and fat, you remain the most handsome man in our tribe. I've enjoyed their envy."

Disa had the grace to look guilty, but Soren chuckled.

"We are two of a kind. I have often thought much the same. You are still the most beautiful woman in this clan, and I am the only man who has known your body, who has made you cry out in ecstasy. Cry out in just the same way as I will make you do tonight. Over and over."

"Promise?"

"Promise, Dee."

Soren spent the rest of the night keeping that promise. Their coupling was more than a means to release. They made love for the first time as they took their time exploring, pleasuring, and sharing.

FIFTEEN

Ivar's head was on a swivel as he and Jan raced through the trees on horseback. He searched for any sign that Lena and their friends had traveled along that road. He had been certain he and Jan would have caught up to them by now. That they had not, made him fear the worst. Were they still galloping at full speed, too? If they were, what had them so fearful?

"At this rate, we'll get all the way to Kaupang before we catch them." Jan scowled and pushed his dripping hair from his eyes. The rain had let up, but it had drenched them by the short and intense downpour that accompanied them for the first half of their ride.

Ivar had barely noticed the cold and damp, but the rain had made visibility difficult, and sometimes they had to slow to a walk or trot before returning to a gallop. Ivar cursed the weather for slowing them. He only wished it had slowed Lena enough for him to catch up.

"Don't tempt fate," Ivar grumbled.

"The clouds are covering the moon so we might ride past them and never realize it." Jan looked around before releasing an ear-piercing whistle that made both horses whinny.

"Jan," Ivar warned, but before he said more, an answering whistle came. He knew the sound as though it came from his own soul. "Lena!"

Ivar and Jan spurred their horses toward four figures that stepped onto the path. As they drew closer, they saw four bows pointed towards them.

"Lena, put your damn bow down before you shoot me. Again," Jan griped. "I still haven't forgiven you from when we were children."

"I didn't shoot you. I shot the apple."

"That I was biting into!" Jan pulled his horse to a stop and slid from the saddle, running through the mud to embrace his sister. He tucked her under his chin and kissed her head before whispering, "Thank the gods, Lena. I couldn't lose you. You've been sister and mother to me all these years, and I still need you."

Jan stepped back and let Ivar encircle her in his arms. He lifted Lena off her feet as he smothered her words with a kiss. He ignored the others and walked into the tree line.

"He's making that a habit," Eindride groused before calling out, "Don't go too far. We don't know who or what else is out there."

Ivar walked just far enough to give them privacy. He ran his hands over every part of Lena he could reach before cupping her jaw in his large hands and pressing a feather-soft kiss to her lips.

"Not enough," Lena whimpered as she pressed her lips more firmly against his, demanding entry for her tongue. She swiped it against the velvet interior of his mouth as she pressed her body against his.

When they pulled back, they stepped apart. They assessed one another, each for their own reasons.

"I'm hale, Ivar. They didn't hurt me."

"I couldn't do it, Lena. I couldn't."

"I figured that when I realized it was you. You couldn't have made it here so quickly if you'd been with her very long."

"I admit I--"

Lena's hand covered his mouth.

"No. Don't you dare tell me. I don't want to know."

Ivar pulled her hand away before kissing her palm.

"Let me speak. You don't know what I was going to say. I was going to say I admit I should have tried harder for our tribe's sake, but no matter how I tried to pretend she was you, it would never be enough to fool me into bedding another woman."

"You were thinking of me?"

"It was the only way to make my body do anything. It wasn't going to be up to much if I didn't picture you. You're the only one who has ever stirred it."

It shocked Lena that she was about to ask for more details, but now she had to.

"How far did you get?"

Ivar shook his head before closing his eyes. He was incapable of looking at Lena as he admitted the truth.

"I kissed her, and once she removed her nightgown, I touched her breasts. I was prepared to— to kiss her elsewhere, but there was no way to ignore that she wasn't you. I couldn't do that. It was far too intimate. I had a sheath on, but even when the tip of my cock touched her, it was utterly all wrong. I jumped from the bed and lost everything in my belly to the chamber pot before running out. I suppose the only good thing is that I didn't call her by your name."

Lena absorbed what he told her. She felt ill knowing he had seen another woman naked and had nearly bedded that woman, but it was meant to have been far worse. She had prepared herself for Ivar going through with the bedding. Lena eased the breath she had not realized she was holding from her lungs. Part of her wanted to rail at him for touching Inga even a bit, but she knew she had no right, least of all because he was standing there with her and not his wife. She was now the other woman.

"Lena?"

Lena nodded but stared at the ground. Ivar tucked his finger beneath her chin and lifted it until he gazed at her face again.

"I want to be angry. I want to be jealous. And I suppose I am jealous, but I know I have no right. You are supposed to be hers now. Not mine."

"Do you think I would be any different if the situation were reversed? I think you're far more reasonable than I ever would be. You haven't killed Inga. I would undoubtedly kill any man who thought to take you from me."

"Don't fool yourself. The thought has crossed my mind many times. Especially as I shot two men tonight."

Ivar growled as they inevitably came around to the reason they were standing amid a forest.

"I saw the blood in your home and the dead bodies outside. Your father and Jan were there when I arrived. I had no idea anything had happened until Einar arrived, saying Brenna sent him."

"What? No. Brenna couldn't have sent him. She remained in the mead hall to make it look as though she wasn't aware that Eindride and I planned to go together. She's the one who warned Rangvald and Lorna."

Ivar shrugged, "Maybe she saw him in the mead hall and thought he would be the best person to send to me."

Lena's skepticism still showed on her face, but she let the matter go. She had noticed Einar seemed to grow more scheming and manipulating. She had not liked him much when he was a child, but she always assumed it was because he wanted to be like Eindride and Ivar but was too young to keep up. Now, she suspected he resented what Ivar and Eindride had accomplished. He made her uneasy, but Ivar and Eindride trusted him and were willing to foster him as a warrior.

"What do we do now? You can't remain here with me, and I don't want to go back yet." Lena looked over her shoulder to where their friends waited. "I think you have to go back."

"I know I do, but I'm not going without you."

Lena shook her head. "No, you need to go back, and Eindride will accompany me to Kaupang. He's already told me he will stay long enough to be sure I'm settled with my aunt and uncle."

"I will see you settled." Ivar crossed his arms and cocked an eyebrow, but his bravado faltered at Lena's dismissive eye roll.

"Eindride is more like your brother than just your friend. Do you not trust him to protect me?"

"I trust him just fine. I just don't trust anyone else. We have no way of knowing who else may be sent after you. You and Eindride can only fight so many people at once. You fought two in your home, but Rangvald and Lorna had already dealt with three others. The more people you have on your side, the more likely we are to keep you alive."

"Well, you and Rangvald can't stay away. You must go back to your wife, and Rangvald needs to be with his family. Lorna will go with him, I'm sure."

"Nay, I willna," Lorna's voice floated through the mist until Lena and Ivar spotted the small frame. "I agree that Ivar and Rang should return, but I dinna think Lena and I should. Ulfhild and Inga will only be too glad to see the hind side of me. Neither of them likes me, so they will think they had received a boon if they've chased us both off. But if ye and Rang dinna return, then Thor and Jarl Soren will be forced to send warriors to bring ye back. I dinna think that will end well for anyone. It's better if ye go back on yer own while Eindride and I travel on with Lena. Jan can come with us if he wants."

"No!" Rangvald's booming voice cut through Lorna's suggestion. He, Jan, and Eindride joined the other three, moving their conversation to the trees. "Absolutely not. You are not going anywhere without me. You haven't been here long enough for some trader not to capture and sell you. I'm not losing you because some slave trader thinks you'll bring him a good price."

"Ye think Eindride or Jan would let someone sell me off?"

"I think you are too beautiful for anyone's good, and I'm in a better position as a jarl's son to keep my bride with me."

All heads swiveled toward Rangvald who stood with his hands on his hips. Rangvald's brow furrowed as he took in five faces with varying degrees of surprise.

"What?" Rangvald demanded.

Lena, Ivar, Jan, and Eindride shifted their gazes to Lorna whose eyes shot sparks of anger at Rangvald.

"I don't think Lorna appreciates your lack of confidence in her ability to defend herself," Jan whispered.

"I believe she's capable of defending herself, but just like Ivar would feel better with more swords arms to protect Lena, I feel the same about Lorna. And who will question my right to keep my bride even if she is foreign. I'm a jarl's son. The son of one of the most powerful jarls in the Trondelag."

Lena laughed and shook her head before offering Lorna a look of sympathy.

"I amnae worried aboot some slaver trying to take me away. Let them try. I'd like to go back to this business of yer bride. I didna ken ye had one, Rang."

"Of course, I have a bride. You. Who are you talking about?"

"I wouldnae ken since nay one has asked me to marry them."

Rangvald opened his mouth then snapped it shut before doing it once more. His bashfulness was endearing as he rocked on his heels.

"I suppose I should have asked you, but I assumed you understood. Lorna, I want you for my wife."

"That's nice."

"Lorna, that's nice? That's all you have to say?"

"Aye. Ye told me what ye want, but I dinna recall ye asking me if that's what I want."

"Isn't it?"

"Yes. But ye still havenae asked."

Rangvald looked around the group before looking back at Lorna. "Didn't I just ask you?"

Lena laughed again and stepped closer to Lorna, wrapping her arm around her friend's waist.

"You admit that you assumed she would marry you, and you even asked if she wanted to, but you haven't actually asked if she will."

"Why would I when we're already in agreement that it will happen?"

"Because she's a free woman."

Rangvald stepped forward and opened his arms to Lorna who walked into his embrace and encircled his waist before resting her head against his chest.

"I'm sorry I've gone about this backwards.

Lorna, I love you. I have since the day we met. I've made a mess of this entire courtship, but I can't live without you. Marry me, my love. Please."

"Aye." Lorna reached up on her toes and kissed his jaw before stepping back to Lena's side. "Now, that ye ken I will marry ye, ye can head back. Jan, Eindride, and I will bring Lena back in a few weeks when we ken it's safe."

Rangvald huffed, but Ivar's quelling look made him bite his tongue.

"Congratulations, my friend. I'm happy for you and your bride, but we still haven't resolved what we shall do for my bride." Ivar looked at Lena. "The one I want."

"Eindride and Lorna travel with me to Kaupang. Jan goes back with you and Rangvald. You can send him when it's safe for me to return."

The sound of pounding hooves cut their conversation short. Their horses whinnied and stomped their hooves, only to be met with answering neighs from the approaching riders' mounts.

"Get the horses off the road," Ivar pushed Jan ahead of him as they ran back to the group's mounts. "Get Lena into the trees."

Ivar stood in the middle of the road, Rangvald joining him while Eindride stood just off to the side, his sword drawn. Lorna and Lena hid among the trees, their own swords in hand. More than two score horsemen reined in. The leader crossed his arms as he leaned over the horn of his saddle.

"Ivar, Rangvald. Your fathers are none too pleased at your disappearance." Magnus Ragnorson looked at Eindride. "And I'm particularly displeased with you, Son."

Eindride attempted to not let anyone see him swallow as he looked at his father, Jarl Soren's second-in-command. His father happened to be the largest man in their tribe, and while he was a gentle giant most days, his temper was that of legends. Eindride preferred not to cross his father.

"Magnus, you know why we left." Ivar spoke up. "But as you can see, I found Rangvald and Eindride, but I wasn't successful in finding Lena."

Magnus's expression showed they had not fooled him.

"You found the two men who accompanied your woman but did not find your woman. And in the meantime, did you lose Jan and Lorna, too?"

"Lorna and I had a fight, and she said she'd rather take her chances returning to our home than ride another mile with me," Rangvald interjected.

"Jan insisted on taking off to find his sister. We were just trying to decide where Rangvald should look for him while Eindride and I search for Lena. Rangvald and Lorna were too busy arguing and Eindride was too busy listening to notice Lena slipped off." Ivar cast the dirtiest look he could muster at his friends.

"And where are the horses we heard? Did they just disappear, or is someone holding them for you in the trees?" Magnus looked past the three young men, but the fog sat too low and too heavy for him to see very far.

"We took them away from the road since we didn't know who approached."

"You didn't know who approached yet you stepped into the middle of the trail." Magnus pointed the fault in their claim before dismounting. "I think we shall take a little look to see if we can help you find your wayward women."

With a nod of Magnus's head, the warriors from both tribes dismounted and slipped into the trees on both sides of the road. Ivar, Eindride, and Rangvald held their breaths, unable to intervene but awaiting the inevitable discovery. As the minutes ticked by and no alarm was raised, the three friends dared exchange glances as they tried to keep their faces impassive. Magnus came to stand in front of his son, and Eindride struggled not to squirm.

"Tell me true, Ein. Where are the women?"

"I don't know. If they were nearby, the others would have found them. I don't know where they've gone." Eindride was relieved he did not have to tell his father a lie.

"Where do you think they've gone?"

"Away from Inga," Eindride whispered to his father. "Do you know why Lena ran?"

Magnus nodded as he cast his gaze at the warriors who had accompanied them.

"Lena is being accused of murder. Inga claims that just like she has bewitched Ivar, she did the same to Inga's guardsmen. Inga is shouting from the rooftops that Lena seduced them men into following her like a siren, then Lena killed them to leave Inga defenseless and unprotected. Jarl Thor is supporting his daughter after Ivar failed to consummate the marriage. Soren had no choice but to send riders out. You can see that many of them aren't even our people. They're Jarl Thor's. Soren's hands are tied, and so he has ordered we bring Lena back to face the accusations and trial."

"You must know how ridiculous that is," Eindride whispered.

"We all do, but with no one in the village to defend Lena, there are only people to support the lies. Without Rangvald and Lorna there to admit they killed three of those men in Lena's defense, there is no one who can exonerate Lena. It's not enough that Tormud claims the men followed and attacked Lena. Even Soren can't speak on her behalf since they will expect him to oversee the public trial. Lena must come back to defend herself."

"You know Ivar will never agree to that. She is already as good as dead. We may as well burn her alive for the justice she will receive. Rangvald won't return without finding Lorna, and neither will Ivar return without finding Lena. The best I can offer is me returning. I can tell what happened."

"But you weren't at Lena's longhouse. Brenna is in danger too, Ein."

"What?" Eindride demanded.

"They're holding her as a conspirator. You all need to return. This isn't something that will blow over just because Lena stays away. Inga is out for blood."

Eindride looked back at Ivar and Rangvald, who listened to the conversation between father and son.

"Go back, Ein. Help Brenna," Ivar nodded.

"You know I would stay with you if I could, Ivar." Eindride looked at his father before looking back at Ivar and Rangvald. "She's carrying our first child. We planned to wed within the moon. I can't let anything happen to her."

Eindride watched the scowl soften on his father's face, even if for only a moment. Magnus pulled his son into his embrace and whispered in his ear. "If you have to leave with Brenna to protect my grandchild, I will help you go tonight."

The sound of a man's scream rent the air before a deeper one sounded. Warriors flooded the trees as Ivar and his friends joined the force rushing toward the sound of swords.

Ivar's heart lurched as he watched Lena fend off a warrior from Thor's tribe who focused on maiming or killing as opposed to subduing. Lena's blade sliced across the man's ribs, shredding the flesh, but the warriors seemed unfazed. If anything, it galvanized the man into a rage of wild thrusts and parries. Ivar raced forward, impaling the man through the back as Lena's blade severed her opponent's arm.

Ivar spun as a blur shot past him, recognizing Rangvald as he leaped at a man who had a handful of Lorna's hair wrapped around his wrist. Lorna cursed as she was pulled to the ground along with her attacker when Rangvald tackled the man. It was only a heartbeat later that the sound of breaking bone echoed off the trees, and one of Ivar's clansmen lay with a broken neck.

"Cease!" bellowed Magnus. The older warrior came to stand between Ivar and Rangvald. "If the lot of you don't return, the feud this farce of a marriage was meant to end will explode in our faces."

Lena joined them as she wiped blood from her face and shook out her arm, which stung from the flat side of a sword blade striking it. She looked around at the damage from the brief skirmish and accepted that Magnus was right. She may have wanted to run to Kaupang, but her absence would not solve a matter that far exceeded her relationship with Ivar or the tantrums of a spoiled young woman. The mix of warriors were eager to use fighting over Lorna and Lena as an excuse to fight one another.

"I'll return," Lena conceded. Before Ivar responded, she turned to him. "We have to trust your father. You said he knows you shouldn't marry Inga. We have to believe he will see things through for the betterment of our clan, and if he knows that means Inga must leave, then she will."

"But will that be before she kills you?" Ivar growled.

"Only the gods know that. I can't hide if it will cause a war between our clans. We must resolve this through good faith rather than swords." Lena whistled, and Jan stepped from the trees with the horses.

She mounted before Ivar argued and nudged her horse next to Magnus. "Do I return as your captive?"

"I'm afraid so. I won't bind you, but you must turn yourself over to Soren."

"Thank you, Magnus." Lena turned towards her friend, a weak smile and tired eyes greeted him. "Eindride, I didn't know about Brenna. You have my congratulations and my apologies for bringing her into this. I will do whatever I can to ensure no one blames her for any of this."

Ivar tied the reins to his horse to Lena's saddle and mounted behind, pulling her back into his embrace. She sank against the warmth and comfort of his broad chest as he wrapped his protective arm around her middle as though he could create a barrier between Lena and the world that seemed out to get her.

"I'll ride with you most of the way," Ivar's words comforted Lena that he would not leave her on her own, while reassuring Magnus that he would not ride into the homestead flaunting that he chose Lena over Inga.

SIXTEEN

Ivar could not help but believe the entire attempt to whisk Lena away had been a colossal failure. He was happy for his friends—Lorna and Rangvald were now betrothed and Eindride would be a father—but Lena was no safer. She was in more danger than ever before, and he felt even more incapable of protecting her. His arms wrapped around her snugly as she rode before him. She had said nothing since he mounted behind her and they set off. The tension cascading from her was like waves in a tempest, but she was the most dangerous of storms; the kind that was silent until it unleashed its wrath. While Ivar trusted Lena's judgement, he did not trust that she would not attempt to shoulder all the blame to protect him from his father and Jarl Thor. Her mind was ticking, but he had no idea what she was thinking.

"Don't fret," Lena's whisper cut into his thoughts. "I won't do anything rash. I will see what the jarls have to say, and I will accept the voice of our people."

"No." It was a simple statement, but Ivar hoped it conveyed his unwillingness to accept anything less than Lena being found innocent and then being made his bride.

"What do you mean 'no'? There is no other option." Lena continued to whisper. She looked at those riding near them and sensed that warriors from both clans were curious about what she would do and what they discussed.

"I mean I am not turning you over to my father or Thor, and I don't trust people to believe your side of the story."

"Then you don't trust our own clan's members, people we have known our entire lives."

"That's right. I don't trust them because if I could, we would not be riding home. I would be seeing you to your aunt and uncle. If Magnus is telling the truth, and of all people why wouldn't he, then our very clan members are clamoring for your blood just like Thor's are. It means they have already decided that siding with Inga is more entertaining."

"Or they understand that not angering the woman who will one day be the frú is a healthier choice if they wish to have a long life."

"She won't be frú."

"Ivar, you can't still think your father will put her aside after all this, do you? You can't possibly end the marriage now that Inga has cried foul. She will make it seem as though you are trying to kill her, too. It's one thing for her to blame me, the jilted mistress, but if you try to end this, then she will claim you are plotting against her and her tribe. She has neatly backed you into a corner from which you can't run."

"Then I will make her want to leave." Ivar's gruff voice had a finality to it that Lena learned as a child was not worth fighting. They finished their ride in silence until it was time for Ivar to move to his own horse.

. . .

The riders cantered into the homestead and reined in where Soren, Disa, Thor, and Ulfhild waited. Ivar spotted Inga standing with Signy and Torbin, but his attention was refocused when five of his father's guards dragged Lena from her horse and threw her to the ground. She remained there for only a moment before easing to her feet, a knife in each hand in case one of the men thought to push her down again.

"I will go willingly." Lena looked at Soren and dipped her head before looking at the guards. "But push me again when I can walk on my own, and you will draw back a hand short."

"How dare she?" screeched Inga. "Who is she but a whore? How dare she issue orders when she should be thrashed for attempting to have a jarl's daughter killed?"

Inga rushed forward and tried to push past the guards, but the tone shifted with her intrusion, and the men now became Lena's protectors. They formed a circle around Lena and kept Inga from striking.

"Who tried to kill you?" Ivar boomed. "It could not have been Lena. She was too busy trying to keep *your* five warriors from killing her. Are you saying there are others here who don't want you?"

The collective gasp was deafening. Soren marched over to Ivar and grabbed Ivar's arm, steering him toward their longhouse and refusing to look anywhere but straight ahead. Ivar seethed with his own anger but allowed his father to maneuver him. He looked over his shoulder and cast a knowing look at Eindride. His best friend was already standing beside Lena with Lorna and Rangvald now protecting her too. The crowd followed father and son to the gathering hall, leaving Lena behind.

Ivar breathed easier knowing there was not a

mass of people waiting to harm her. He had spoken out hoping he might draw the attention away, and it had worked. Now he needed to figure out how to keep Lena from being shackled to the *niðstöng*. If they tied her to the shame-pole, she would be subject to the elements and the scorn of both tribes. The weather was pleasant during the day, but the nights had turned, and winter was rapidly approaching. Snow flurries had already hung in the air more than once in the past weeks.

"You are committed to ruining this alliance, aren't you?" Soren hissed in Ivar's ear.

"No. I already told you that Harold, Rangvald, and I are on good terms. We can make this alliance last for generations without this marriage."

"But it's too late. While you were off riding about the countryside, Harold has forsworn your agreement since you shamed his sister. He is refusing to honor any type of truce once he is jarl unless you remain married to Inga. Thor is ready to murder you in the name of his daughter's honor, and it wouldn't surprise me if Inga and Ulfhild don't poison you. And while you might deserve all of that for being such a fool, you will get Lena killed. My hands will be tied if our people decide she's guilty. You have made it obvious that you believe she is above the law and that you will shelter her from any accusation of wrongdoing."

"Those accusations didn't come until after she fled to save her life."

"That isn't the timeline your bride is claiming, and her parents support her."

"And you're allowing Inga to gain control. She will soon think she can control this entire tribe if her caterwauling gets the attention she wants. She is a young woman about to bring this tribe to its knees."

"And if her husband had been around to control

her, she wouldn't be out of your bed long enough to say more than your name." Soren's grip tightened on Ivar's arm as he thrust him into Ivar's usual seat at the head table. "You abandoned your bride to run off with your mistress. How could you have imagined this wouldn't be a disaster? Oh, wait. I would venture to say you didn't think. You want me to believe that Lena would make a better frú for this tribe than Inga, but you won't be able to keep Lena alive long enough to prove it."

Ivar opened his mouth, but Thor stole his chance to answer when he swept in with his family on his heels. Inga's smile was smug as she took her seat next to Ivar and entwined her arms around his.

"You might have been able to warm your cock between her thighs if you'd done right by me, but now you will never have her again," Inga purred into Ivar's ear. "You picked the wrong woman, and now you will make it up to me. Embarrass me again, and I will ensure her death is brutal rather than done quietly and cleanly."

Ivar yanked his arm free and stood to his full height. He picked Inga up from her chair and hefted her over his shoulder before turning toward his chamber. He stormed towards the door that would lead to the family chambers, not looking back.

"My bride and I have lost time to make up." Ivar's hand rained down a heavy spanking before mercilessly pinching Inga's backside. Inga squirmed and tried to wriggle free, but Ivar's hold was far too tight. "You wanted my attention, wife. Now you have it."

Ivar marched to his chamber and kicked the door open. He heard Ulfhild and Thor following him, but he slammed the door shut before anyone followed them inside. He dumped Inga on the ground and barred the door. Ivar placed his hands on his hips and towered over Inga, but she showed no signs of fear or submissiveness. Instead, she scrambled backwards until she stood beyond Ivar's reach. He did not follow her but curled his lip in disgust when she sneered at him.

"You may not want me, Ivar, but you have me. My father won't allow you to end this marriage. I won't allow you to end this marriage. I deserve to be a jarl's wife, and I intend to become one. You would do well to remember which tribe is stronger."

"Someone has filled your head with pretty little lies if you believe it is yours. If you believed that, why would you be in such a hurry to remain here, to become the frú of a weak people? You know it's your tribe that is benefitting by having us accept you. Don't forget that with any bride comes a dowry. Do you think it is you or the dowry that is wanted? You couldn't get my prick up, but you are still here. I know which one I want."

"Perhaps your prick doesn't work at all, and that's why you ran. You'd rather hide your lack of manliness by claiming you want your little slut than admit that you can't perform."

Ivar's laughter bounced off the overhead beams and the walls. The sound filled the room, mocking and antagonizing Inga as his look of pity grated on her nerves.

"Every person in my tribe has seen my body's reaction to Lena. It's no secret. More than enough people have heard if not seen us coupling. Everyone knows my cocks works. When it wants what's offered." Ivar stepped toward Inga, but the young woman dodged away. His laughter once more rung out and filled the chamber. "What? Not interested in seeing if you can change my mind? Not interested in seeing if you can seduce me?"

Inga paused as she looked at Ivar, trying to determine if he was mocking her or offering her a chance. She raised her chin and glowered at him before stepping in front of him. She pressed her body against his before cupping his groin. Ivar stood still as she ran her hand over his rod, but nothing changed. Inga stepped back in disgust, her pretty face turned sour as she looked at the bulge in Ivar's pants. It was no more noticeable than any man's resting cock. Nothing had happened when she attempted to arouse him. Ivar's laughter once more mocked her as she spun around and rushed for the door. Ivar's longer legs carried him there faster, blocking her reach for the bar.

"Oh, no. You and I shall remain here until you can prove to me why you want to stay. So far, you can't claim it's because I want you, nor can you claim that I can satisfy you. You say you deserve to be a frú, but there are any number of tribes you could marry into to do that. You want me to believe that you are doing me a favor by becoming my wife; however, that makes little sense if power is what you want. If you won't admit you don't want to stay because of pride, then you shall live a life of humiliation if you stay here. I will never touch you. They will scorn you as a failure as a woman if your husband won't bed you. If you fall pregnant and everyone knows I won't fuck you, then they will label you a whore and your children killed. You will be nothing here. So once more, why do you want to stay?"

Inga lashed out, her nails scraping along Ivar's cheek as her fist drove into his groin, causing him to double over. Ivar lurched forward, knocking them both to the ground. They landed in a tangle of Inga's skirts with Ivar between her legs, his cock resting against her mound. Inga stretched, trying to rub her mons against him. Her immediate arousal made Ivar's brow quirk. He realized she would have acquiesced to any demand, her pupils dilated, her hips straining, and her fingers digging into his backside as she whimpered. He palmed her breast, squeezing it before using the pad of his thumb to circle her nipple.

"Even when I mistreat you, you still want me," Ivar murmured near her ear. "But I don't think it's me who you want. You just want any man who will pleasure you. And that makes you an even more worthless wife. I can never trust that you aren't letting other men leave their seed within you. You can't fight to defend my home. You'll never care for my people more than you care for yourself. And you're more likely to fuck my friends and my enemies than you are to be loyal unto just me. And that is why, Inga, you will return home."

Inga tried to push Ivar from her, but the more she moved, the more she slipped toward release, her body reacting to her closeness to a man. While Ivar's body remained disinterested, Inga's hungered for his continued contact. She closed her eyes as she strained to move her mons against him. Ivar froze and let Inga do what she wanted until a gasp and a sigh signaled Inga had found what she needed.

"Perhaps I should be flattered into thinking you desire me that much, or perhaps I should be intrigued by a woman whose body is so highly responsive. But instead, I have already told you I will never trust you. So, let me now explain what will happen." Ivar grasped both of Inga's arms and lifted them over her head, pressing his weight against her as she whimpered. He rocked his hips, knowing that he had complete control over her.

"You will retract your accusations against Lena. You will remain in this chamber except for meals. You will not speak to anyone other than your family. If I discover you have had any visitors other than your family, I will kill whoever it is. You make it clear to your father that you want this marriage to end and that you want to return to your home. If you attempt to leave this chamber or convince anyone to help you leave, I will beat you. You want to be my wife, well, now you get to live as such. You are my possession to do with as I please. You are not your father's daughter any longer."

"You are not a man who beats women. Everyone knows that."

"No one knows any such thing. I have been with one woman in my life, and I love her. Who is to say how I would treat other women? You should heed Rangvald's warning. You don't know what my temper is like. If you prefer not to find out, then do I say. If you don't like this arrangement, then convince your father to leave. But either way, you want to be my wife for now, so you will have to live the way I demand. And no one can say otherwise."

"I am a free woman. I have my rights."

"Exactly. Leave if you don't like it. But if you stay, then you agree to this marriage on my terms. I am the man in this marriage. I can do as I like. And what I'd like is to not see nor hear from you, nor do I wish for anyone else to see or hear from you."

"You would make me the prisoner when it is your whore who's locked up." Inga regretted the words as soon as they left her mouth. The look in Ivar's eyes would surely freeze her blood.

"You have a poor memory. I just told you, you will retract your accusations. Lena will be free. She has no husband, so she can do as she pleases. You, on the other hand, do, and you will do as I tell you."

"My father will never stand for this." Inga fought in truth to get free of Ivar, and with little effort, Ivar rolled away from her.

"Then tell him it's time to go home."

"Never," Inga spat at Ivar's feet.

"Very well." Ivar walked to the door without looking back. He stepped into the passageway and locked the door, pocketing the key. He heard Inga's curses as she banged on the door and rattled the handle. Ivar walked back to the gathering hall with threats of the gods forsaking him at his back.

SEVENTEEN

Lena looked around the village square, huddled into herself as she attempted to block the wind from further chilling her. She had not seen Ivar since he left her with Eindride, Rangvald, and Lorna. When Ivar and his family, along with Inga and hers, went into the jarl's longhouse, the guards had overpowered Eindride and her friends, dragging her to the *níðstöng*. Members of the village she had known her entire life heckled her and lobbed insults at her. Children threw spoiled and rotting vegetables at her while the guards shackled her to the post. She refused to look away, forcing each person to look her in the eye as they tormented her. Her silent calm unnerved many, but a few continued to antagonize her.

Jan had gone to fetch their father when they rode back into the village. Tormud brought blankets and furs for her, but the guards had refused to allow her to take them. Rangvald stepped in, and it was only the fear that the skirmish between tribes would start again that convinced the guards to defer to Rangvald's orders. Despite the misery of being cold, filthy, and humiliated, Lena refused to overlook the fact that she was still alive. Soren could have had her killed the moment she returned, and Thor could have demanded any number of types of justice for the alleged crimes. So, while she shivered and stank, she was grateful that she was not already dead or being tortured.

"Lena."

Lena twisted around to see Ivar running toward her. He was almost within arm's reach when guards stepped out to block his way. Eindride pushed away from the wall against which he had been leaning.

"Ivar, you can't." Eindride came to stand in front of Ivar, blocking him Lena's view. "We have to wait to see what the jarls decide. If you interfere now, it will only make it worse. She's safer here than anywhere else. No one can get near her without anyone and everyone seeing. You have to wait."

"She's freezing, Ein. How can you think I'm going to walk away?"

"Because you have to. Let the tribe see she is strong enough to endure this. The whole point of fighting for her to be your wife is because you love her, and part of the reason you love her is that she will be a leader people will talk of for generations. She has to prove that on her own now. Let people see in her what you always have. There's no choice but to let this play out now. Let the people see her endure with strength of mind and body while Inga wallows in pity and accusations. Let the people see the true difference between them. They will decide what is right. But if you swoop in, you will make Inga look like the ill-used bride and make Lena look like little more than a bed warmer."

Ivar ran his hand through his russet hair and shook his head as he looked past Eindride's shoulder. His friend was right. Nothing was going as it should. Ivar could not have imagined even if he had tried that he would ever see Lena manacled to the shamepole, nor could he have imagined that defying his spiteful bride would have put the woman he loved in such jeopardy. Ivar had gravely underestimated Inga, but he would not make the same mistake. He had already found Rangvald and Lorna on their way to look for Lena and Eindride. Ivar explained to Rangvald and Lorna what he intended to do with Inga, and he had placed guards outside his door and windows to ensure it was impossible for Inga to leave. He selected men who would not betray him. Ivar chose men who feared their wives cutting off their bollocks if they succumbed to Inga's attempts at seduction. He arranged for Einar to ferry reports to him from the guards. Ivar would keep Inga in virtual house arrest until Thor agreed to end the marriage.

"I still need to speak to her. I need to hear for myself that she is all right. I won't leave without doing so." Ivar tilted his head as he looked at his best friend. "Wouldn't you do the same if it was Brenna?"

Eindride nodded and stepped aside. Ivar crouched before Lena, pulling the furs more tightly around her shoulders. He pushed hair away from her face before cupping her cheek. He noticed the blue veins beneath the surface of her cold lips. Ivar brushed his own warm ones against hers before pressing a kiss to her chapped lips. Their mouths fused together as they gave and took strength from one another.

"I will get you free of here as soon as I can. I will not allow this to go on." Ivar whispered against Lena's lips.

"Do what you must for the long haul, not just what you think I need right this minute." Lena's lips stung as she spoke, the dry skin cracking further. "I will survive out here. We have both been through far worse. Do you remember when we were ten, and we raced Eindride across the frozen fjord? He and I made it, but you were too heavy. The ice cracked sucking you in before we reached you. Ein and I got you out, but then I lost my balance and fell in. I got stuck under the ice and couldn't find the hole. You and Ein pulled me free, but then the ice splintered too much for us to walk back. The three of us sat shivering together for an hour before our fathers found us. I have no idea how we didn't freeze to death, but my backside has never been warmer than after the paddling my father gave me. We survived that. We will survive this."

Ivar nodded, his smile sad from the memory and from Lena's attempt to reassure him. He felt like a failure that it was Lena who was the one being kept a prisoner, who was bolstering his courage instead of the other way around.

"I will make all of this up to you, my love. I promise you that. I locked her in my chamber. I've made it clear to her and to the guards at the door and windows that I do not allow her out. She can see her family, but otherwise, she remains in there. If she wants to be my wife that badly, then she will have to decide if she will live here by my terms. If her father wants her to be my wife, then he will have to accept that she is mine to do with as I want."

"Ivar," Lena warned, but he shook his head.

"How else can we be rid of her? She has to decide that she wants to leave on her own. I understand that."

"I hope you're right."

"Me too, Lena." Ivar looked around and noticed people watching them. "I have to go, my love. I don't know when I can or should visit. I will speak to my father about having you moved inside. Inga knows she's expected to recant her lies that you tried to have her killed and that you seduced her guards."

Lena nodded before squeezing Ivar's hands. She had noticed people watching them too. She swallowed her whimper as Ivar walked back to his family's home. Lena looked over at Eindride, who smiled sympathetically. When Brenna arrived a few hours later with a large bowl of *skouse* that was still hot enough to burn her tongue, Lena was certain the gods would smile upon her. But the sun dropped beneath the horizon, and they left her chained to the *níðstöng*. Exhaustion caused her to drift off, but she stirred when she sensed someone sat beside her. She opened her eyes and found Lorna wrapping a large plaid around them both. They huddled together, their bodies sharing the minimal heat they each mustered.

"Rangvald doesn't think his father or mother will agree to leave with Inga right away. They will insist that Ivar just needs time to get accustomed to marriage. Rang fears what they may demand as your punishment. He thinks Ivar's plan to keep Inga locked away will be enough to wear down Thor's insistence that Inga remain here. Thor's spoiled her for too many years to expect her to behave as a woman should. Thor will have to accept that he made her into a woman who is too weak to lead."

"Do you think he will admit that?"

"Not out loud, but she will force him to when she sends messenger after messenger complaining that she is being ignored."

"Don't you fear that this will fail? I do. I fear how Ivar treats her will anger Thor, and this will only lead to a greater war."

"Then he shouldn't have married her to him. Marriage here is not so different for a woman than it is in the Highlands. Once we wed, we become the property of our husbands for them to do with us what they want. The only difference, the good difference, is a Norse woman can leave her husband. A

Christian woman is bound to her husband until death."

"That sounds horrid."

"It can be. That's why I intend to make the most of a Norse marriage to Rang. That way I can leave if I must. After all, you only live once, so you may as well enjoy it."

"No, you don't. You can live more than once." Lena's brow furrowed in confusion as she thought about Lorna's comment.

Lorna laughed, "You only live once at a time then. Perhaps, there is something to be said for your Norse faith."

The next two days seemed to drag on as everyone existed in a state of misery. Lena remained locked to the shame-pole, while Inga remained locked in Ivar's chamber. Ivar refused to step foot in that wing of his family's home, instead bedding down in the gathering hall. Thor tried to demand that Ivar allow Inga freedom to at least roam about the jarl's longhouse, but Ivar only shook his head. Ulfhild threatened Ivar and started a fight in the gathering hall when she lobbed insults, first at Ivar, then at Soren and Disa. Ulfhild questioned both men's manhoods and claimed Disa did nothing to intervene in the situation because she was jealous of Inga. Harold attempted to push their sparring beyond just training and received a gash across his thigh for his recklessness. It was Rangvald who wielded the sword that injured Harold when he intervened as his older brother tried to decapitate Vigo. Tension was escalating between tribes and among clan members.

It was Signy's voice of reason that offered a chance for peace. Signy suggested that her family return to their homestead and that the additional attention would only continue to make it hard for the newlyweds to settle into married life. Regardless of what Thor and Ulfhild thought, they had married their daughter off, and now she needed to live as a married woman. When asked whether the gods told her it was time for Thor's tribe to leave, Signy would only answer with her own question: why would the gods want them to stay if the marriage was the means to a truce not a merger? The idea of the two tribes blending into one was enough to make Thor's people pack.

Four days after Lena's arrest, Thor, Ulfhild, Rangvald, Lorna, Sven, Signy, and Harold, along with their warriors, rode away from Soren's home. Ivar had not seen Inga once since he left her locked in his chamber. He had heard things being shattered and thrown, but he did not care enough for any of his possession to enter the chamber and talk to the shrew who now warmed his bed alone. Instead, he bedded down in the gathering hall but slipped out when the other people who claimed spaces began to snore. Ivar met Tormud each night and donned the man's cloak. He tucked his russet curls under the hood and went to sit beside Lena. He held her against him as she shivered, trying to look more like a father comforting his daughter than a man protecting his lover. They barely spoke, fearing someone would recognize Ivar despite how he attempted to limp to convince people he was Tormud.

The moment they no longer saw Thor's party on the roadway, Soren ordered guards to release Lena. Soren had sworn to Thor that he would hold a trial to determine Lena's innocence, and he was honor bound to keep his word. It was the first time Ivar allowed Inga to enter the gathering hall. She spewed her bile about Lena attempting to have Inga's personal guard killed to make it easier for Lena to murder Inga. She attempted to make Lena sound like the jealous and jilted lover, but Inga came across as a pitiful young girl begging for attention. Ivar barely spared her a look as he sat beside his father. She had not recanted her accusations, and he had no tolerance for her. There was little chance for him to speak on Lena's behalf, but Eindride and Brenna did, along with Jan and Tormud. Several other members of the clan stepped forward to vouch for Lena's character. When the tribe cast their votes, no one raised a single hand beside Inga to condemn Lena.

Once Lena's innocence and freedom were ensured, Ivar permitted Inga to leave her chamber during the day. Soren assigned her to Disa, who oversaw Inga's work within the kitchens and around the longhouse. They afforded Inga the courtesies of being married to the jarl's heir, but Ivar rarely spoke to her. They sat beside one another at each meal, but Ivar spoke to Eindride and Vigo or the other men who sat at the next table over.

While Ivar stood beside Magnus and Eindride at Eindride's wedding to Brenna, it was Lena who stood with Brenna, not Inga. It was Lena who took Brenna's *kransen*, her maiden's crown, when she and Eindride retired for their wedding night. Lena and Brenna had been close before this ordeal, but Brenna was not a shieldmaiden. She had always remained at the homestead when Lena and the other warriors traveled. However, Brenna's steadfastness made Lena realize she had missed an opportunity to have a friend. They grew close while Soren had Lena chained to the *níðstöng*. When Lorna left, tears wetting her eyelashes as she clung to Rangvald, Lena had been certain she would be alone. She understood it was only safe for Ivar to visit her in the dark of night, but it was Brenna who brought her each of her meals, and it was Brenna who kept her company while Brenna sewed clothes for her unborn babe. Lena realized that Brenna was showing already, but she had been too involved in being a warrior to notice. She envied Brenna's connection to Eindride, a permanent tie that could never be severed even if one day they separated. Lena wondered if she would ever know what it would feel like to carry the child of a man she loved.

Once Lena was free to return to training, she focused on regaining the strength she lost in less than a week of being chained outside in the elements. It shocked her that she did not grow ill during that time. She resumed her duties around the village but avoided the kitchens where Inga spent most of her days. She oversaw the women who worked in the laundry and the dairy, helping whenever she could. The village was not sure what to make of the two women who vied for the role of the next frú. They knew Lena to be a quiet but determined worker, while Inga complained about everything, but it was Inga who claimed the title of Ivar's wife.

During this time, Ivar and Lena abstained from making love. They barely touched each other except for the nights Ivar kept Lena from freezing to death. Snow had already fallen daily, and it blanketed the ground by the time Lena moved back to her family's home. Tormud and Jan whittled about Lena, who withdrew further into a shell while working herself to exhaustion each day. Ivar noticed the lines that were forming around Lena's eyes from the strain. Despite not seeing her bare, he noticed she was losing weight that her slender frame could not spare. He encouraged her to eat whenever their eyes met in the gathering hall, but Lena had no appetite. Inga, on the other hand, ate with vigor despite doing half the work Lena or the other women did. Inga seethed when Ivar was nearby; a healthy fear had developed despite her rage. She did not put much past her husband if she pushed him too far. She realized she had made an error in insisting her father marry her to Ivar. Now her goal was to return home and find a better man to marry.

"Shh. You can't let anyone hear you," Inga murmured as Einar entered through the window. Ivar had eased the guard to just two warriors outside the door. Inga thought him a fool for assuming the cold weather would keep her from running away. His belief only made it possible for Einar to slip into the chamber every night. Since no one took an interest in her once she retired, she was able to continue her affair with Einar.

"Are you issuing me orders when it is you who would caterwaul every time you find your release? If I didn't muffle your cries, everyone would know that you're being fucked. And not by Ivar."

"Then you shouldn't stir me to such a frenzy." Inga purred as she pressed her body against Einar's. "If you didn't pleasure me so well, I wouldn't lose control."

Einar pulled Inga against his body, thrusting his hardened shaft against her mound. He pulled the tunic from Inga's shoulder as his hand slid beneath the neckline and his fingers grazed her nipple.

"But you do so enjoy how I fill you with my cock. Your quim hungers for how I fuck you, doesn't it?" He pinched her nipple to the point where tears pricked behind Inga's eyes. "How would you like me to take you tonight, my love?"

Inga understood the game Einar played with her. It had developed over the weeks, and she knew that he did not care what her answer would be. He would do with her as he wanted, and that was what she wanted.

"I'd like you to hurry is what I'd like." She cupped his manhood as she pulled at the laces to his leather pants.

"Giving orders again. You do like to test me. I shall show you that the only one who gives orders is me. You may do as you like with the thralls. Order them about all day, but you shall do as I tell you. Touch yourself, Inga, once you strip. I would watch you as I undress. Then on your knees."

Inga hurried to follow Einar's commands, already feeling her body hum with excitement. She was certain she loved him. She did his bidding, loving how he brought her hours of exquisite pleasure but craving how he took command. He left her not needing to think or worry about how to make people obey her or respect her. She understood she did not have the power to make people like her; she had given up as a child when she realized that everyone would always revere her sister Signy while they overlooked her. With Einar, she was wanted and loved, and so she submitted to each of his orders, her mind and body hungering to submit to their depraved love play.

Inga slid her fingers into her sheath and panted, making sure to not make a sound that someone might hear beyond the door. She kneaded her breasts as she watched Einar strip off his boots then leather pants. She sank to the floor, her knees wide when she saw his cock spring free. It was long, with more girth than any other man she had been with. She was aware of the dew dampening the inside of her thigh. She arched back, presenting her breasts to him as he slid his cock between then. She bowed her head, lapping at the tip each time it pressed toward her lips.

"I hunger for your honey, Inga. Get on the bed."

Einar slapped her backside, making sure to graze her nether lips. He flicked his finger inside the swollen flesh. "Already so wet."

Einar laid back on the bed as Inga positioned herself, so they both enjoyed the wonders of their mouths. Einar's fingers bit into her flesh, his nails leaving crescent marks on her ample backside while Inga's lips wrapped around his sword. Her hand stroked him as she suckled his rod. Einar closed his eyes as he inhaled her scent, the musky flavor filling his nostrils and making his cock twitch.

He had not intended to fall in love with Inga, only wanting her to become dependent on him, but he did indeed love her. They had talked in between their rounds of lovemaking, and he realized she was more intelligent than he assumed. She had a keen and conniving mind that he was glad was on his side. Once it was obvious that Ivar would not bed her, they had taken care for him not to spill his seed inside her. Rather, he found a sense of warmth and tenderness when he saw it spill across her skin. He wanted her to himself, even if he had to accept that he would never marry her. The dichotomy between her cunningness and submissiveness intrigued and beguiled him. But despite accepting that he loved Inga, it was Lena's face that flashed before Einar's eyes, and it was her name he had to swallow, each time he found his release.

It frustrated Einar that Inga's position was doing nothing to further his goal to grow closer to Ivar, and thus Lena. He had tried to offer his help to protect Lena during the nights she was stuck outside, but it was Ivar who always went to her. He had offered to be a silent and discreet guard, but Lena and Ivar rejected it, telling him it was unnecessary. Even when his brother shut himself away with his bride for their honeymoon, they had not accepted Einar's offer. His anger and bitterness found their outlet in Inga. The angrier he came to her, the greater their climaxes. She was a drug to him as much as Lena was. He was not sure that he could survive without either of them.

"Enough. It's time for me to be inside you, my little love slave."

The first time he had referred to her as such, Inga had lost her temper. It was the only time she ever rebelled, but Einar had been quick to subdue her, proving that she was, in fact, his slave since she did his exact bidding and her body gave her little choice.

Einar pressed her flat onto her belly and covered her with his body, his weight trapping her against the mattress as he slipped inside her. Their fingers entwined as he rocked against her. He kissed the exposed skin of her neck as he crooned nonsense in her ear.

"Einar, please," Inga begged as his thrusts began to speed up. "Just this once."

It was the same refrain Inga had uttered ever since Einar began pulling out before he climaxed. One hand came across her mouth, smothering anything else she might have said. He slid his hand to her throat, the fingers enclosing around her and squeezing. He halted his thrusts as her body trembled beneath him.

"Would you like to go without, my sweet? I shall fulfill my needs, but I can leave you longing."

Inga tried to shake her head, but her neck and the weight on her back kept her from moving. "Then be a good girl. Can you do that for me?"

Inga relaxed and pushed her hips up once again offering herself. Einar shifted onto his knees and rammed into Inga as hard as he could. He hammered into her until she sobbed in silence, her need more than her mind could withstand. When her inner muscles spasm around him, he welcomed his own release as it creeped over him. He pinned her backside to his hips as his rod twitched over and over within her.

When their climax ebbed away, Einar pulled Inga into his embrace, arranging them on the bed then drawing the covers over them.

"You listened to me," Inga's hushed tones held awe as she gazed up at him, the reverence and submission clear for Einar to see.

"I did, my love. I am still determined that you shall carry my children. One day our son shall be a jarl."

Inga's eyes widened as tears seeped from the corners. She shook her head as she burrowed into Einar's chest.

"I've sent my father missives almost every day. I have next to no guardsmen left to carry them anymore. And yet there is no sign that I shall leave here. Even if I do, who will I marry to grant you that wish. How will I see you?"

"That last concern is for me to worry about. I have heard that Hakin Hakinsson needs a bride. I could sail to Steinkjer often, with few people wondering where I have gone. I have proven I'm a good fisherman, and I like to sail alone. I may be young, but I have been going to sea to fish since I was barely more than a boy. I'd visit you there."

"I have heard the man is half crazy with ambition. What if he discovered you, us?"

"With his ambition, do you think Hakin would admit that his wife cuckolds him? Do you think he would tolerate anyone knowing he can't satisfy you and that you turn to another man? No, he will keep silent if he ever learned. He has too much pride. Even if he wanted to kill you for it, it would mean people would know. What woman would go to him after that? A wife killer who can't fuck."

"You seem so certain."

"I am."

"I wish I was able to ask Signy what future she sees for us."

Einar squeezed the thigh draped over him and shook his head.

"She probably already knows, but as long as she says nothing against us, then we can't ask. If she interferes, she won't live long enough to tell us or anyone else anything."

"You'd kill my own sister? No, Einar. No. That I can't agree to. Promise you will never harm my brothers or sisters. For better or worse, they are my family. I do love them. I love Signy best of all. It's not her fault she has a gift, and while everyone pays all their attention to her, she has taken care of me. I'm not a good sister, and I realize that, but she has still loved me. And for that, I love her."

Einar sensed Inga growing agitated, so he stroked her hair until her eyes began to droop. Her breathing slowed as she once more burrowed into his chest.

"I won't hurt your family, but family is not enough to stop me from one day creating a legend people speak of with awe."

Einar never let himself fall into a deep sleep with Inga, fearing someone would discover them, but he relaxed and enjoyed having her next to him. He was not as convinced as he would have her believe that their saga would be one of the great ones, but he would die trying to make it so.

EIGHTEEN

Lena looked around the sparring circle and sensed eyes upon her. She was certain it was not Ivar, although he had been keeping a closer eye on her since their return, even with Thor's departure. As long as Inga remained in the homestead, neither Lena nor Ivar were convinced she out of danger. She swept her gaze across the warriors who were still fighting until she noticed Einar standing off to the side. She had not shared her suspicions with anyone, but she thought Einar and Inga might be having an affair. They were a similar age, and Einar had changed since Inga arrived. He seemed both calmer and more calculating than before. The young man had made her uneasy for years since she found him staring at her with unmasked lust, but she had hoped that as he grew into manhood, he would find a woman to ease his unspent energy. The only thing that kept Lena from being sure that he was coupling with Inga was how he still looked at her. Lena shifted to see if his gaze followed her. It surprised her when it did not. She glanced behind her to see who Einar was watching, and a smile twitched at the corner of her mouth to realize he had been watching Inga walk across the village center. He had not been watching

Lena after all. She sighed with relief until Einar's gaze locked with hers, and he smirked as if he read her thoughts. He turned away, and Lena looked back to see Inga watching them. The hatred in the young woman's eyes was enough to make Ivar appear by Lena's side.

"She seems to hate you even more than she did when she arrived. She has to have heard that we haven't been together since before the blessing." Ivar watched Inga slip into a storage shed. Lena and Ivar stood together long enough to watch Einar slip into the same building a few minutes later. "Do you believe they are having an affair?"

"Yes." Lena's answer was simple and without doubt.

"Then there is my reason to have her sent home."

"What will you do about Einar?"

"Nothing. They are both young. He's hardly more than a boy and filled with lust. She is attractive and lonely. It doesn't surprise me that they found each other." Ivar looked down at Lena, unsure how she would react to him acknowledging Inga was pretty.

"I can see why she draws men's eyes. She is beautiful in a way that is far different from how I look."

"But you still know that it's you I crave, don't you?"

Lena looked up at Ivar and saw the hesitation, the nervousness in his eyes.

"Do you think I want you any less because we haven't been able to make love? Don't you think I admire you even more for not being able to have you? Ivar, I'm not worried that your interest wanes."

Lena caught herself before she laughed at the relief that flooded Ivar's face. She was not about to admit she had feared that exact thing. The longer they spent unable to be together, the more she worried that he would realize he did not need her. She feared that he would find another woman, even Inga, who would be available to him.

"Lena, there will never be anyone else. Don't try to fool me or yourself that you don't fear we are drifting apart. I worry about it constantly."

"But we're not?" Lena's voice was little more than a breath escaping her lips.

"No, we aren't. I'm going to my father now, and I am coming to you tonight. I'm not going another night without sleeping with you in my arms. And trying to keep you from turning into an icicle did not count."

"We can't. Not until Inga leaves."

"No. No more. I am not married to her. This was a trial, and it has failed. The blessing was to guide us as we attempt a marriage. We were never wed."

"See what Jarl Soren says first."

"I don't care what he says. The winter solstice will be upon us in a few weeks. I will be married to you then, or we leave."

Lena nodded and then squeaked when Ivar pulled her in for a searing kiss. It was the first one they had shared since Ivar found her alongside the road. Lena melted against him, her will to resist nonexistent. At the cheers of those around them, they broke apart.

"Kiss! Kiss! Kiss!" The chant went up as the warriors still surrounding them beat their swords against their shields as laughter filled the air.

Lena and Ivar looked around, shocked by their friends' and fellow tribe members' encouragement. It was the most lighthearted they had heard their people since before Thor arrived with his family and with Inga. Ivar was only too happy to oblige. He swooped in and gathered Lena into his arms as he pressed a tender kiss to her lips that snowballed into a fire of need between them. As the kiss drew on, the applause and bawdy comments were deafening. When they pulled apart at last, they rested their foreheads and the tips of their noses together, their smiles clear to everyone.

"About damn time," a woman's voice called from the crowd.

"Praise Freyja. They've come to their senses!"

Ivar and Lena brushed their lips together one last time before stepping apart. As they turned to look at the people who stood watching, they both noticed Inga standing outside the storage hut. Lena stiffened until she saw the young woman nod her head. Lena only stared. Inga's attitude was so different from only minutes earlier when she glared with open malice. Lena wondered if Inga's anger was in part because she was still stuck in limbo. Now Inga would have the evidence needed to either have Lena banished or killed, or she had reason to leave. Lena prayed it was the latter.

"She wants to leave," Ivar whispered. "I saw the difference, too. She may still make trouble, but I bet she will demand an end to the trial."

"I hope so."

With a quick hug, Ivar turned toward his family's home. Ivar was determined to speak to his father. He would not wait any longer to send Inga home. He had taken ten steps when a scream filled the air and gasps echoed. Ivar spun around in time to launch himself forward and catch Lena as she pitched forward, an arrow protruding from the center of her back.

A blazing fire erupted in Lena's back as something pushed her forward. She stumbled, and would have fallen if Ivar had not sprung forward and caught her. She whimpered as she bumped against his chest. The fire spread along her left side all the way down her arm and leg while her head floated several feet above her. The edges of her vision seemed to tunnel into a tiny pinprick before her eyes.

"Ivar," she mouthed before everything went black.

Ivar clung to Lena as blood flowed from the wound in her back. He scanned the crowd but was unable to catch a glimpse of who shot the arrow. He supported Lena as he tried to decide what to do, but his mind was running through sludge.

"Take her to your mother," Magnus appeared at his side, helping him lift Lena into Ivar's arms, but Ivar was too stunned to move. "Hurry, Ivar. Wake up!"

Ivar shook his head and looked down at Lena's pale face. His feet began moving without him realizing. Magnus jogged alongside him, supporting Lena's legs.

"Who?" Ivar barked.

"I don't know. I didn't look, but I believe they caught someone. Once I help you get her inside, I will go back to find out what happened."

Ivar remained silent as they entered his family's home. He turned toward his chamber but remembered that it was now Inga's space. He would not take Lena there; Ivar intended to never step foot in the room again. He went to the room Lena had occupied while Lorna stayed with them. Vigo had gone in search of Disa and Soren as soon as the arrow flew toward Lena.

"Gods, what happened to the girl?" Disa swept into the room.

"Someone shot her, Mother."

"I can see that, but how? Lena would never be

reckless enough to walk into the archery range while people are shooting."

"We were in the sparring field. We weren't anywhere near the targets. Someone did this on purpose."

"Any idea who?"

Ivar turned at the sound of his father's voice, but looked down at Lena before shaking his head. He had placed her on her stomach on the bed. He snapped the shaft from the arrow before moving aside to allow his mother space to work. Father and son stood together as they watched Disa cut away Lena's tunic and vest. Soren grasped Ivar's shoulder when the wound became visible. It was deeper than it had appeared when Lena's clothes covered it. The arrowhead had sunk deep into her back close to her backbone and her heart. It was a miracle she had not died the instant the arrow struck her. Lena sobbed as Disa attempted to pull the tip free. Despite being unconscious, Lena's whimpers were clear and tore through Ivar. Soren wrapped his arm around his son and turned him away from the scene on the bed. Father embraced son, just as he had countless times when Ivar was a child. Ivar wanted to look but could not. He could not bear seeing Lena with an arrow sticking out of her back. They had seen each other injured before, but never had a wound been this serious. Ivar feared Lena might never walk or move her arms again if she survived the loss of blood.

All heads turned when the door opened, and Brenna entered with Eindride at her side. Brenna went to help Disa as they whispered back and forth as they worked.

"It was one of Inga's guards. They caught him as he jumped from the stable roof. The guard had the bow in hand and claimed responsibility. He said that he saw the way Lena humiliated Inga by kissing Ivar in public. The man was duty bound to defend Inga." Eindride explained. "I don't believe it. More than one person saw him come from the barracks before going to the stables. There was no way he had seen Ivar and Lena before going on the roof. They already planned this."

"That's why Inga went in the storage building. She didn't mind someone seeing her with Einar if that meant no one blamed her for sending her guard. She planned that, too." Ivar muttered.

"What? What's this about Inga and Einar?" Soren interrupted.

"Lena and I saw her enter one of the storage buildings and a few minutes later Einar followed her. Lena suspects they're having an affair. Even if they're not, she wanted us to see her. She wants to go home, but not before she punishes Lena."

"Do you think anyone else knows if she's having an affair?" Soren wondered.

"Ask the guards who've been outside her door. No one has reported anything to me, but if she is, I'm sure they've heard her. Ask Einar himself." Ivar shrugged. He did not care whether or not Inga was still coupling with other men. Ivar was only interested in Lena's condition. He went to kneel beside the bed and took Lena's hand. It seemed so tiny and limp in his palm. He looked up at his father, and Soren knew where the blame rested without Ivar saying anything.

Ivar, Soren, Eindride, and Vigo, who had arrived with Soren, waited in silence while Brenna and Disa worked to clean and stitch the wound. They had just finished when Tormud and Jan arrived. Ivar realized it had not taken the women long to work even though it seemed like an eternity had passed since he and Lena were kissing in the village center.

"I'm sorry, Ivar, but I can't allow Lena to remain

here. Jan and I are taking her to Kaupang. We're moving there." Tormud voice rasped as he stood behind Ivar and looked down at his daughter. She was the image of her mother, and so much like the woman he had adored. They had not been married nearly long enough before he became a widower. The idea that his daughter would die from another woman's scorn was intolerable. He hated watching Lena go off to battle, but there was glory in that.

"We can't move her," Ivar's voice broke.

"Not now, but when she is well enough."

Ivar shook his head. "When she is well enough, I'm marrying her. I already told her it would be by the winter solstice. Father, that bitch better be gone before the sun rises tomorrow or she will be dead before it sets."

The finality in Ivar's tone warned anyone from trying to dissuade him. Brenna went to stand with Eindride who ushered her from the chamber while Disa stepped into Soren's embrace. Ivar had barely looked at his father since Lena's arrest, so he had not noticed that his parents' entire relationship had shifted in the past weeks. It floored him to see his mother rest her head against Soren's shoulder and how tenderly his father held her. Jealousy tightened his throat, angry that his parents had a chance while he might never see Lena open her eyes again. Tormud and Jan pulled chairs over to sit on the other side of the bed from where Ivar still knelt. He was not even aware of the tears that streamed down his cheeks as he prayed to every god he hoped might intervene and keep Lena from leaving him.

NINETEEN

It was late the day after Lena's second attack that Einar cupped his hands for Inga to step into. He mounted his own horse and nudged it forward as he led Inga and the handful of men who were the remainder of her personal guard through the gates. He had convinced Soren and Ivar that he would be the best person to take Inga home. Since he was Magnus's younger son and the only one who would travel, he argued that they could trust him not to kill her once they were beyond the homestead walls. Neither Soren nor Ivar brought up the possibility that Einar was bedding Inga. Neither man cared so long as she left. Soren barely kept his tribe from stoning Inga when it became known that not only was Lena injured but it had been at the hands of one of Inga's guards. The man who fired the shot was already a corpse that the wolves had torn apart the night before.

Inga rode out with none of the attention paid to her when she arrived. She had been a constant source of tension. Everyone was aware of the pain the situation caused Ivar and Lena, but Inga had been awkward and unkind to everyone she encountered. She had attempted to exercise more authority than she had. She had even disagreed with Disa in public on more than one occasion, attempting to insist her way was better than the experienced frú's. Disa had tolerated her for her husband's and son's sakes along with their tribe's, but she detested Inga just as much as everyone else. She had always hoped Lena would one day replace her, and now that she was on better terms with her husband, Disa had shared just how better suited Lena was. Soren and Disa spent many nights lying in bed talking after making love, something they had never done before. They had always rolled over and gone straight to sleep, or at least pretended to, but now they discussed their tribe's future. They had to send Inga home, and they needed Lena to marry Ivar. Disa and Soren also accepted that they would have to trust Ivar to ally with Harold and Rangvald.

Unfortunately, the weather broke within an hour of Inga's attempted departure. There was no option but for them to turn back. Einar was unwilling to risk Inga's life, and he made another sound argument to Soren. If Inga died while traveling home after being rejected, it would undoubtedly spur Thor into a rage. Soren drew the line in allowing Inga to return to his home. Ivar had publicly renounced her, and the agreement to a trial marriage ended. He had been tempted to insist Magnus and his family take Inga in, but he did not want Einar and Inga spending any nights under the same roof. He sent Inga to stay with two widowed sisters and ordered her to remain sequestered away. Her last days in Soren's homestead would be like her early ones, locked away and out of sight. He had wondered if he was being too harsh, but his daily visits to see Lena confirmed he made the right choice. Soren watched as it was Ivar's turn to waste away. Ivar ate little while Lena fought a fever that did not release its hold for more than a week. Disa shared in private that she feared Lena might never awaken if the fever continued to ravage Lena's weak body.

It took a fortnight before the weather cleared enough for anyone to attempt to travel. When someone shook Ivar, he was ready to swing his fist before he realized it was Rangvald who stood beside him.

"I've come to collect my sister and to offer my apologies. Words can't express my regret and hurt that Lena has suffered at my sister's hands. Ivar, I don't know what more to say."

Ivar looked up at his friend's tired face, and he took in Rangvald's travel-stained clothes. Movement caught his eye, and he glanced over to see Lorna sitting on the opposite side of the bed. Ivar had slept in the bed beside Lena once his mother said it would not harm her. Lorna perched on the edge and was whispering to Lena.

"Thank you, Rang. This wasn't your doing. You and your sister are different people. You aren't to blame."

"I bring other news. Ivar, my father and Harold are dead."

"What?" Ivar could not believe what he was hearing. "How?"

"Harold was on patrol on our northern border when cattle thieves attacked. He thought to take on the lot of them instead of waiting for me and Sven with some of our other warriors to encircle them. My father did not die with such glory. He caught an argue and didn't recover." Rangvald glanced at Lorna then Lena. "A fever took him."

Ivar nodded as he continued to watch Lena. Her hand was once more in his, just as it was most of each day. He had done everything to care for her, refusing help from anyone but his mother and Brenna.

"Ivar, I don't think you realize what this means." Rangvald waited for Ivar to look up, but when his friend did not, Rangvald continued. "I am now jarl. Our alliance is through me, not my father, not Harold, and certainly not Inga."

Ivar nodded but he could not muster any relief knowing Rangvald would not hold him to the marriage. He could not stir any well wishes for Rangvald.

"Lena, ye must wake up. I need ye to be there for ma wedding. Rangvald says he has a different plan, but I insist ye must be there." Lorna squeezed Lena's other hand. "If it werenae for ye and Ivar, Rang and I might never have admitted we love each other. I saw what ye have with Ivar, and I wanted it, too. If ye hadnae let me stay here, I would have run even further away. Besides, Signy says we will be a family one day. Ye have to live to make that happen."

Ivar looked up at Lorna's last words and raised his eyebrows.

"Aye, Signy says she will have a lass one day who will be part of yer family. She says she willna be alive to see it, but the gods have shown her for years. She couldnae say aught before, but the lass will wed yer son. A son ye dinna have with Inga for sure. She says she sees Lena beside ye."

Ivar swallowed as he leaned over to kiss Lena's cheek.

"Do you hear that, my sweet one? You have to live. If Signy says it, then it must be true. Though I'm not convinced that marrying off my son before he's born is something I will consider." Ivar scowled as he thought about how Lena came to be so ill. His poorly arranged marriage was to blame. His scowl dropped when Lena squeezed his hand. He looked down to see her lashes flutter. "Did you hear me, Lena? Can you hear me?"

"She squeezed ma hand, too!" Lorna grinned. "Lena? Are ye awake, lass? Really awake?"

"Mmmm," a soft agreement came from Lena as she looked around, searching for Ivar. When he came into focus, her smile was the one Ivar remembered. It blinded him with its brilliant happiness. "Water."

Lena's voice was croaky from lack of use, but she was aware of everything that happened around her. She sipped water as she listened to Ivar and her friends, but she grew tired easily. Rangvald and Lorna were to wed in the spring, and she intended to be there, but Ivar and Rangvald had come to their own sort of alliance. They wanted to use the end of the trial marriage to their advantage. Ivar would speak to his father, but they would maintain the pretense of a hostile truce. Their other enemies and allies would not learn that they were friends in the hopes that they would each gather information their neighbors would not share if they were aware that the two most powerful tribes in the Trondelag had joined forces. They would only come to one another's aid if they truly needed it, but in the meantime, they would share anything they learned that might affect one another. Rangvald and Ivar insisted it was not possible for Lorna and Lena to not attend one another's weddings without the plan falling apart.

Lena managed another smile; this one directed at Lorna. Both women were committed to finding ways to see one another's wedding, even if they did not stand beside one another.

Rangvald and Lorna left with Inga two days later, but it was a month before Lena was well enough to be on her feet. Winter had set in, and by the time the healers gave Lena a clean bill of health to get married, she feared Rangvald and Ivar had been the ones to see the future. She did not expect Lorna to make it to her wedding. It saddened her that the woman besides Brenna who she trusted and liked most would not be there. She prayed she would attend Lorna's in the spring.

TWENTY

"Hurry or you will be late to your own wedding," Brenna laughed. She rubbed her rounded belly as she watched Disa finish braiding Lena's hair while the bride herself struggled to pull on the fur-lined boots that were a wedding present from Ivar. Her shoulder twinged with pain as she strained, but she felt better than she had in weeks. She and Ivar had finally been able to move forward with their wedding plans; knowing they could wed on the winter solstice had motivated Lena to recover quickly. She had been a model patient and recuperated faster than anyone expected. Tormud wanted her to move home once she was well enough to leave the jarl's longhouse, but Ivar had been adamant that she remain. The chamber she occupied was now theirs, and he joked that he was afraid she would slip away if he did not keep her nearby.

"I don't envy Ivar having to go digging for that sword. I'm happy to have my father hand me his dagger," Lena laughed as she pictured Ivar, digging through snow and dirt at the catacombs for the ancestral sword Soren buried at his birth for the wedding ritual. She did not find anything boyish about Ivar anymore, except perhaps his smile. If she could have rescued him from the rite of passage that supposedly made him a man, she would have done so.

Lena looked down at the rings in her hand and smiled as she remembered her mother wearing hers. Her father's eyes had shone the night before when he passed along the set of rings he had exchanged with her mother all those years ago. She traced the intricate scrolls on the metal, and it made her think of the tattoo on Ivar's arm. She recalled how he had gritted his teeth and born the pain of the serpent being painted into his skin several years ago. He and Eindride had received matching tattoos just before their first voyage as captains. She had wanted one too, but Ivar had talked her out of it, saying he could not imagine anything marring her skin. She should have known then that he was attracted to her, but it had taken a drunken kiss for them to both realize their shared feelings. That night seemed both ages in the past and only a moment ago. Her heart pounded as she realized that this day would be the beginning of a new set of memories that only she and Ivar would share. She wondered about the children she would one day bear and what their life would be like once they led their tribe together. She prayed that they would have a long and happy life together. Her parents' time had been cut short, and while her father had a companion to ease his loneliness, she was certain he would never remarry. She did not want the marriage Soren and Disa had for so many years, and while she did not truly think they would, a small fear resided in the back of her mind that she and Ivar might one day drift apart. She pushed that aside as Disa finished decorating her hair with ribbons. She wished the weather permitted flowers for her hair, but she was unwilling to wait for something so trivial to marry Ivar.

They were marrying on the winter solstice, the

longest night of the year. Brenna had teased her that Ivar picked this day so he had time to make up for their nights apart. It was nearly sunset, and their ceremony would take place as the sun dipped into twilight. After the marriage vows would be the ritual solstice celebration, then a feast to celebrate the two occasions. She and Ivar had already agreed they would escape as soon as no one would notice. Lena wanted to run away the moment Thor's hammer was placed in her lap, using the fertility ritual as an excuse to appreciate the gods' good will. Ivar had begrudgingly convinced her that they should not do that as the future jarl and frú, as their people were expecting to celebrate with them for longer. He agreed to leave after the first pitcher of mead was gone. Lena suspected that would be within the half hour after they were seated at the feast.

Lena spotted Ivar through the crowd as she approached the altar. It was not difficult to do since he was one of the tallest men in the village, but she was also drawn to him like a loadstone. She could have spotted him among the densest mass of people. As she approached, a slight movement near the trees caught her attention. She looked over in time to catch a glimpse of a small cloaked figure climbing into the tree followed by a large one. Two sets of shining teeth told her that Lorna and Rangvald had joined them and were smiling to share their well wishes. She and Ivar had done the same thing only weeks earlier since Rangvald decided he would not wait until spring to make Lorna his wife if Ivar was to make Lena his bride that winter. Lena had threatened to travel alone if Ivar tried to refuse her. Her heart had ached that she was unable to stand closer to her dear friend, but she had been filled with joy when she saw how happy the couple was to be wed at last.

Now her friends shared in her excitement. When she met Ivar's gaze, she tipped her head minutely toward the trees, and Ivar nodded. He had seen Rangvald and Lorna, too. The ceremony proceeded in a trance-like state for the couple, both aware and dazed at the same time. The rest of the world slipped away into a blur, but their eyes locked and never shifted as they pledged themselves to one another. Electricity flowed between them as they recited their vows and exchanged the rings Lena slipped onto the hilt of Ivar's new sword. It felt like the briefest of moments before the village shaman announced they were wed. The cheers that went up were the loudest that had been heard at a wedding in generations. The merriment was so unlike the dismal acceptance of Ivar's trial marriage. People had cheered then, because it was expected. These felicitations were heartfelt.

Ivar removed Lena's *kransen* before he kissed her, refusing to be rushed as he absorbed the taste, scent, and feel of his bride. He had dreamed of this day since he came into his manhood and realized that he craved Lena in a way that far exceeded friendship. He knew then that they were destined for one another despite the trials they had experienced. They had spent so much of their time avoiding admitting their love aloud, but now he would never waste a day professing his feelings. He would tell her morning, noon, and night.

Lena and Ivar joined hands and moved aside as the *Jól*, or Yule, celebrations commenced. Pitchers of a strong fermented ale passed through the gathered tribe, and the toasts celebrated the beginning of *Jólablót*, the three-week season of Yule Sacrifice. The shaman donned the skin and head of a goat and lifted a live one onto the altar, drawing his knife quickly across the animal's throat. He thanked the mighty Thor for protecting their people and the coming sun. The blood was caught as it drained over the side. As the newly married couple, Lena and Ivar were the first to dip their fingers into the basin. They drew lines along each other's nose and cheeks. While Lena disliked knowing it was blood that stained her skin, there was something erotic about painting one another as they gazed once more into each other's eyes, the rest of the world fading away.

"May the gods look favorably upon us for the new year. May our dead rejoice in their feasting with Odin in the golden hall of Valhalla and may those who feast with Freyja in Fólkvangr enjoy the fruits of the goddess's harvest. Let the light of spring come forth from this night forward," the tribe's priest intoned the blessing.

As if summoned on demand, the sky burst into the blue and green hues of the aurora borealis. The light jumping and dancing as it shimmered across the darkening backdrop and the first stars began to twinkle. The majesty of the night was not missed by Ivar and Lena. It was a fresh beginning after their weeks of misery and separation.

"Let the Sun goddess, Sól, return from the belly of the wolf who stalks through *Hel*. Let the dying and fading of the gods cease as the Maiden returns to us. Let *Asa leika*, the lover of all the gods, bring forth the fruit that fortifies god and man. Give the gods their strength and immortality while blessing us with a bounteous harvest."

With the blessings concluded, the tribe moved to the jarl's longhouse, where bright logs already burned in the hearth, chasing away the darkness of winter. A boar turned on a spit, a tribute to Frey and Freyja and a reminder to Lena to pray once more for fertility. Lena and Ivar took their places at the head table, with Eindride sitting beside Ivar. Lena smiled at Brenna, who sat next Eindride's other side. Further down was Vigo with his wife Yrsa. She was a quiet woman with kind eyes and an easy smile. Lena returned the young woman's smile and promised herself that she would make time to get to know the woman better. They had not seemed to have much in common since they were children, but they often worked in the kitchens together.

"Do you think that All-Father will make an appearance on his mighty steed Sleipnir?" Eindride laughed.

"Since I am yet to see Odin or that monstrous eight-legged beast, I doubt it. Besides, I don't intend to be looking outside tonight." Ivar waggled his eyebrows as his hand settled high on Lena's thigh beneath the table. His fingers caressed the flesh of her inner thigh, and he felt her shiver, his cock hardening in anticipation. It was not long before the mead began to flow, and Ivar stood to make a toast to his bride, removing his Thor's hammer necklace and placing it in Lena's lap.

Lena blushed as their tribe celebrated with anticipation a birth in the summer. She hoped she would not disappoint the people, even if she was not sure if she was ready to give up being a shieldmaiden in exchange for motherhood. After losing her own mother, the thought of giving birth terrified her. The tables had been rearranged for the solstice feast, and as the games began, Ivar nudged Lena. He gathered two jugs of mead and nodded toward their chamber. Lena eased from the table and slipped to the edge of the room before passing through the doorway. Ivar was soon on her heels. She pushed open the door, and they hurried in before anyone noticed their departure. Lena dropped the bar into place, making it impossible for anyone to enter without their invitation.

"Finally," Ivar breathed as he set the jugs onto the table. When he turned around, Lena stood naked before him, having stripped away her gown. He sucked in a breath as his heart stuttered. He had missed Lena during the weeks they had been apart, and even though they reunited before the wedding, he felt starved of her touch. He opened his arms to her, and without hesitation, she slipped into his embrace. Their bodies pressed together, igniting their need. In silence, Lena helped Ivar undress before sinking to her knees. She cupped his bollocks as her tongue flicked over the leaking tip of his cock. She hummed as she encased his stiff rod with her plump lips. Her head bobbed as Ivar laced his fingers through her hair. Her eyes drifted closed as she took him further into her mouth with each pass. He was racing too quickly toward release.

"Lena, it's too much. I want you too badly. I'm not spilling yet." He pulled away to her mewl of protest. He bent and lifted her into his arms. "I intend to make love to you over and over again tonight. There will be time for everything, but right now, I can't ignore my need to touch you, to feel you against me."

He placed her upon the bed as though she were fragile and precious, adoring the way she looked with her blonde locks swirling about her shoulders. He crawled over her, his hand kneading her breast as he bent his head, his warm tongue lapping at her nipple before suckling. Lena did not try to soften her moan of pleasure and desire as he tweaked her other nipple before once again massaging the aching flesh. Her breasts hung heavy and full as she pressed them upward for more of Ivar's ministrations. Ivar shifted to run his other hand along the outside of her thigh to her hip before caressing the smooth skin of her belly. They both watched as his hand rested briefly over her womb before his fingers disappeared into her sheath. Ivar's groan matched another moan from Lena. The feel of any part of him within her making them both frenzied. Lena's thighs fell open wide as Ivar settled fully between them, his fingers working the other set of plump lips, his thumb rubbing deep circles on her bud. She writhed beneath him, needing far more than his questing fingers offered. He found the spot deep within her that made her explode, a wave cresting and crashing over her.

"There is nothing more beautiful in this world or the next than watching you find your release and knowing I gave that to you." Ivar murmured as he lowered his mouth to hers. The kiss took on a life of its own as Lena's fingers combed through his hair before sliding over his back to his buttocks. She grasped the hard muscle that flexed as he rocked against her. She found the grooves in his hips that were made for her to cling to as he thrust into her.

"Gods. That moment when you enter me. I don't know that I can hold on for much longer." Lena tipped her head back as she tried to slow her body's reaction, but it would be futile. Ivar would make her climax again and again, but after the first release with him buried deep within her, she was able to control her need. They eased into a rhythm as his sword surged into her sheath again and again, and she raised her hips to meet him each time.

They chanted one another's name as though they were invocations, reverence infused into each utterance. They rolled as Ivar pushed up and wrapped his arm around Lena's middle, bringing her on top. She sat up as she rode Ivar, the sensation different as he pressed deeper within. It was as though she were floating as she rocked until another climax engulfed her. Ivar watched as the concentration morphed into bliss, his fingers digging into her backside as he pressed her into a quicker pace, his own hips jerking upward as he pushed her over the edge, wanting to claim her once more. Lena collapsed forward, her mouth seeking his, her breasts trapped between them. The feel of her body stretched across his was more than Ivar could withstand. Breaking the contact with her lips, he roared his climax as he once more flipped them. His thrusts were nearly painful as they finished together.

Breathless, Ivar was careful not to suffocate Lena as he lowered his body to hers. They both knew they would cling to one another after such an earth-shattering experience. They always did. Their need to remain close, affection blossoming, was inevitable as Lena stroked Ivar's back. He ran his hand over her hair then temple and cheek before gliding along her neck to her shoulder and arm, finally reaching her hand where their fingers intertwined.

"I love you more than the air I breathe and the life I possess." Ivar whispered.

"You cannot love me more than the life you possess as ours are now one, forever one." Lena smiled, and the softness melted Ivar's heart all over again.

"You're right, my love. Just as our bodies are one, so are our souls. But they have been our whole lives. Now nothing can separate that."

It was not long before their bodies once more demanded satisfaction. Ivar kept his promise, and they made love throughout the night just as they had for years. But they both sensed there was a new dynamic, a new power to their coupling. It was as the early dawn light filtered around the window furs that they drifted off, but their sleep did not last long as they woke one another to join throughout the day. Hunger drove them to open the door several times over the next week, but only the thralls who delivered the trays saw them. They surrendered to the comfort of their love nest, and their family was wise not to interrupt. When they emerged, it was clear to all who saw them that they were a couple who would defy any attempt by man, gods, or nature to come between them, their bond invincible.

EPILOGUE

"How could I have imagined I was missing anything? This hurts more than I ever imagined," Lena panted as pain ripped through her belly once more. "It's a lie. This is not like my monthly cramps. This is nothing like it. I still fight and work with those. This makes me want to rip my own belly open and pull this babe free."

"I know, Lena. We have been through this ourselves, but in a few hours, you will hold your babe. Your son, if we believe Signy from all those years ago." Disa wiped the sweat from Lena's brow.

"Hours! No. I can't. Not without Ivar. Where is Ivar? He promised," Lena whimpered as pain once more threatened to tear her asunder. "What if—what if I can't? What if—again?"

Tears streamed down Lena's cheeks as she thought of the babes she had already lost, never carrying them beyond a few months. No one had an explanation for why she so easily got with child but could not carry one to the end; there had been several such losses over the first year of their marriage. Now Lena lay in the bed she shared with Ivar, labor pains contorting her face, as she wondered if her husband would return from the hunt in time. Ivar had not wanted to go, but Soren and Magnus had goaded him into it. They teased that he was worse than a mother hen when it came to how protective he was of Lena. Just as she was about to give up hope that Ivar would return in time, the door burst open and a sweat-drenched, livid Ivar stormed in.

"No one came to tell me! I ride in and Einar comes running to tell me you're about to deliver, swearing that I was a louse and shite for a husband." Ivar pushed through the attendants that gasped at his abrupt arrival. The women had silently mocked Lena for believing and for needing her husband. Most would not admit that they wished their husbands were so attentive. "Lena?"

Ivar's face blanched as he looked at his wife, who seemed so tiny surrounded by the pillows and furs that propped her up. Her face was a deep shade of red as she panted in agony. He did not hesitate to shuck off his mud-splattered boots and rip his fur cloak from his shoulders. He tugged his dirty tunic over his head before gingerly climbing onto the bed. Ivar took Lena's hand, and for the first time since they were children, he realized how much smaller hers were and how much more fragile the bones appeared. It was a contrast to how he saw her as a warrior and his spirited bride. Now fear seized him after seeing her bear the pain of losing so many children. That seemed like mere discomfort compared to the agony she appeared to be in now. He rubbed his hand over her arm before tentatively hovering his hand over her belly. When she nodded and covered his hand with hers, he rubbed slow circles around the hardened flesh. She sighed as she eased back, shifting to find his shoulder.

"Wait a moment," Ivar whispered. He pressed Lena forward, and despite her moan of protest, he slid behind her, cradling her between his powerful thighs. Her talon-like fingernails sunk into the muscle, making Ivar wince.

"Brenna, how did you do this? Strian was so big when he was born, and you are so tiny. I'm taller than you, and I feel like this babe shall rip me in half!"

"What choice did I have?"

Brenna smiled in sympathy as she bounced her one-year-old son on her hip. Strian had been a large baby, but his chirping and bubble-blowing cherubic face made it hard to remember how much Brenna suffered bringing her son into the world. Lena looked at Disa, amazed once more that the woman had given birth to four sons. The woman looked as fit as she must have been before she had any children. It convinced Lena her body would never return to the lithe and muscular frame she once had. She even looked over at Frida, her brother Jan's wife, and was mesmerized how she was up and walking, visiting her only a few weeks after giving birth to her own son Bjorn. Frida and Jan's marriage took everyone by surprise. The young couple had secretly courted during the ordeal with Inga, but it was obvious they were a love match and did not marry because Frida became pregnant. That did not happen until the honeymoon.

"What about you, Yrsa? Aren't you scared being here, seeing me like this? Doesn't this make you wonder what you've gotten yourself into?" Vigo's wife had announced only the week earlier that they were expecting their first child.

"Perhaps," Yrsa laughed nervously. "But now what am I going to do? Tyra will arrive whether or not I'm ready. I just count my blessings that it will be a girl. Signy told me so when she was here the last time."

Lena thought about the message she had received from Lorna telling her of her son Erik's birth three months earlier. Apparently, it had not been an easy event. Since then, she received one other missive that reassured her that Lorna had recovered and that life with a babe was not as traumatic as Lorna feared. Lena hoped that she would be like her friend and recover enough to return to training soon. She had missed sparring with Ivar in the last months of her pregnancy, after Ivar had thrown a fit seeing her lift a sword and walk into the training yard. She reminded herself that if Lorna did it, she was determined to recover as well. A message from Signy had also accompanied the last one from Lorna. The seer reminded them of her prediction that the two families would be joined by blood more than once. Ivar had scoffed and argued there was no reason for their families to join when in the past year a secret alliance had proven fruitful. Both tribes benefitted by sharing the secrets their neighbors told but did not expect to have passed along. Rangvald and Ivar had spared one another more than one attack, and Soren was grateful for the peace that his son's and Rangvald's friendship created.

"Aaahhh!" Lena's scream rent the air before she bit down hard on her lip, blood coloring the skin.

"It's all right, my love."

"All right? How about you try doing this?"

"Lena, it's time to push," Disa interrupted. She patted Lena's knees until she was in position. It only took four strong pushes, and Lena and Ivar were staring dumbfounded at their son.

"Leif," Ivar's voice filled with awe as he looked at the tiny figure that rested against Lena's breast. The blond hair was so pale it was white, and his arms and legs so long Ivar had not been sure his son had a body when Disa held him up. "He looks like you, Lena."

"Perhaps my face and hair, but that is your massive body. He is a giant already." Lena stroked the back of her finger over Leif's cheek.

"Leif?" Brenna asked.

"Yes, both of our mother's fathers shared that name," Ivar smiled at Disa, who leaned over to kiss her own son's cheek.

Lena kissed Leif's downy scalp as he nursed, and she rocked him. She looked back at Ivar and pursed her lips for a kiss. It was slow and tender, filled with promise for their future.

Lena leaned back against Ivar as his arms wrapped carefully around her and their baby. She closed her eyes and an image of a young woman danced before them. She looked like Lena, but there was something different about this woman. The bright aura of a defiant spirit shone around her as she laughed at a dark-haired man whose face Lena was unable to see. She knew who she was looking at, even if she was not the one with the gift of second sight.

"Freya," Lena murmured.

"Yes, we are blessed by the goddess," Ivar smiled down at his family, but Lena shook her head.

"Our daughter will be Freya. She will be next. Gird your loins, Ivar. She will be like me, but even more spirited. I suspect our son shall be the easy one."

"A daughter? Did Signy tell you that?"

"I just know. I can see her with my heart already. By this time next year."

"Leif and Freya," Ivar tried out the names on his tongue and found he liked them.

"Leif and Freya with Bjorn, Tyra, and Strian. They will be the next generation of great warriors, and they will be our greatest glory." Lena cast her gaze around the room and saw Frida, Brenna, and Yrsa nod; Leif's gurgles sounded his own agreement. After years of strife and unrest, Viking glory was their new destiny.

THANK YOU FOR READING IVAR & LENA

Celeste Barclay, a nom de plume, lives near the Southern California coast with her husband and sons. Growing up in the Midwest, Celeste enjoyed spending as much time in and on the water as she could. Now she lives near the beach. She's an avid swimmer, a hopeful future surfer, and a former rower. When she's not writing, she's working or being a mom.

Visit Celeste's website, www.celestebarclay.com, for regular updates on works in progress, new releases, and her blog where she features posts about her experiences as an author and recommendations of her favorite reads.

Are you an author who would like to guest blog or be featured in her recommendations? Visit her website for an opportunity to share your insights and experiences.

Have you read *The Highland Ladies Guide?* Learn all the behind the scenes details from my flagship series! This FREE book is available to all new subscribers to Celeste's monthly newsletter. Subscribe on her website.

Get Celeste's freebie

Join the fun and get exclusive insider giveaways, sneak peeks, and new release announcements in

Celeste Barclay's Facebook Ladies of Yore Group

VIKING GLORY

Leif **BOOK 1 SNEAK PEEK**

Leif looked around his chambers within his father's longhouse and breathed a sigh of relief. He noticed the large fur rugs spread throughout the chamber. His two favorites placed strategically before the fire and the bedside he preferred. He looked at his shield that hung on the wall near the door in a symbolic position but waiting at the ready. The chests that held his clothes and some of his finer acquisitions from voyages near and far sat beside his bed and along the far wall. And in the center was his most favorite possession. His oversized bed was one of the few that could accommodate his long and broad frame. He shook his head at his longing to climb under the pile of furs and on the stuffed mattress that beckoned him. He took in the chair placed before the fire where he longed to sit now with a cup of warm mead. It had been two months since he slept in his own bed, and he looked forward to nothing more than pulling the furs over his head and sleeping until he could no longer ignore his hunger. Alas, he would not be crawling into his bed again for several more hours. A feast awaited him to celebrate his and his crew's return from their latest expedition to explore the isle of Britannia. He bathed and wore fresh clothes, so he had no excuse for lingering other than a bone weariness that set in during the last storm at sea. He was eager to spend time at home no matter how much he loved sailing. Their last expedition had been profitable with several raids of monasteries that yielded jewels and both silver and gold, but he was ready for respite.

Leif left his chambers and knocked on the door next to his. He heard movement on the other side, but it was only moments before his sister, Freya, opened her door. She, too, looked tired but clean. A few pieces of jewelry she confiscated from the holy houses that allegedly swore to a life of poverty and deprivation adorned her trim frame.

"That armband suits you well. It compliments your muscles," Leif smirked and dodged a strike from one of those muscular arms.

Only a year younger than he, his sister was a well-known and feared shield maiden. Her lithe form was strong and agile making her a ferocious and competent opponent to any man. Freya's beauty was stunning, but Leif had taken every opportunity since they were children to tease her about her unusual strength even among the female warriors.

"At least one of us inherited our father's prowess. Such a shame it wasn't you."

Freya

Tyra & Bjorn

Strian

Lena & Ivar

THE HIGHLAND LADIES

A Spinster at the Highland Court
BOOK 1 SNEAK PEEK

Elizabeth Fraser looked around the royal chapel within Stirling Castle. The ornate candlestick holders on the altar glistened and reflected the light from the ones in the wall sconces as the priest intoned the holy prayers of the Advent season. Elizabeth kept her head bowed as though in prayer, but her green eyes swept the congregation. She watched the other ladies-in-waiting, many of whom were doing the same thing. She caught the eye of Allyson Elliott. Elizabeth raised one eyebrow as Allyson's lips twitched. Both women had been there enough times to accept they'd be kneeling for at least the next hour as the Latin service carried on. Elizabeth understood the Mass thanks to her cousin Deirdre Fraser, or rather now Deirdre Sinclair. Elizabeth's mind flashed to the recent struggle her cousin faced as she reunited with her husband Magnus after a seven-year separation. Her aunt and uncle's choice to keep Deirdre hidden from her husband simply because they didn't think the Sinclairs were an advantageous enough match, and the resulting scandal, still humiliated the other Fraser clan members at court. She admired Deirdre's husband Magnus's pledge to remain faithful despite not knowing if he'd ever see Deirdre again.

Elizabeth suddenly snapped her attention; while everyone else intoned the twelfth—or was it thirteenth—amen of the Mass, the hairs on the back of her neck stood up. She had the strongest feeling that someone was watching her. Her eyes scanned to her right, where her parents sat further down the pew. Her mother and father had their heads bowed and eyes closed. While she was convinced her mother was in devout prayer, she wondered if her father had fallen asleep during the Mass. Again. With nothing seeming out of the ordinary and no one visibly paying attention to her, her eyes swung to the left. She took in the king and queen as they kneeled together at their prie-dieu. The queen's lips moved as she recited the liturgy in silence. The king was as still as a statue. Years of leading warriors showed, both in his stature and his ability to control his body into absolute stillness. Elizabeth peered past the royal couple and found herself looking into the astute hazel eyes of Edward Bruce, Lord of Badenoch and Lochaber. His gaze gave her the sense that he peered into her thoughts, as though he were assessing her. She tried to keep her face neutral as heat surged up her neck. She prayed her face didn't redden as much as her neck must have, but at a twenty-one, she still hadn't mastered how to control her blushing. Her nape burned like it was on fire. She canted her head slightly before looking up at the crucifix hanging over the altar. She closed her eyes and tried to invoke the image of the Lord that usually centered her when her mind wandered during Mass.

Elizabeth sensed Edward's gaze remained on her. She didn't understand how she was so sure that he was looking at her. She didn't have any special gifts of perception or sight, but her intuition screamed that he was still looking.

A Spy at the Highland Court

A Wallflower at the Highland Court

A Rogue at the Highland Court

A Rake at the Highland Court

An Enemy at the Highland Court

A Saint at the Highland Court

A Beauty at the Highland Court

THE HIGHLAND LADIES ALWAYS

A Sinner at the Highland Court
BOOK 1 SNEAK PEEK

I hate him. I hate him. I hate him. How can he do this to me? How could he pick her over me? That fat sow. Kieran will regret this till the day he dies. He and she both. This is her fault. All her fault. I hate her too.

Madeline MacLeod felt the four walls of her tiny convent cell closing in upon her. Her brother, Kieran, had dragged her from Robert the Bruce's royal court at Stirling Castle and dumped her at Inchcailleoch Priory earlier that week. She refused to accept that any of her words or actions had caused her fall from grace. She'd only spoken the truth each time she told Maude Sutherland how unconventionally curvaceous she was. Why her brother wanted to marry a woman who looked more like a tavern wench than a lady was beyond Madeline.

He just wants a good rut. He'll realize what a dreadful mistake he's made when he takes her home to Stornoway. He will realize that tupping her won't be worth the humiliation of having such a plain-faced, round as a barrel, heifer for a wife. He could have had Laurel Ross!

As Madeline listened to the bells toll for yet another Mass, she grimaced. All she seemed to do was pray these days, but God certainly wasn't listening because she remained at the priory despite her fervent appeals. She kneeled among the other novices, postulants, and nuns eight times throughout the day and night as they followed the Liturgy of Hours. The bells in the background signaled Prime, so she knew it was still very early. She'd already attended Matins in the middle of the night and Lauds at sunrise.

Madeline glanced out the narrow window set high in the wall, thinking that the masons must have designed it so the women couldn't escape. The sunlight, weak and dismal, matched Madeline's mood. When she lived at court, six o'clock in the morning was an hour she'd never seen. Now that she lived at the convent, she'd already been awake for an hour and a half.

Madeline dragged herself from her cot and her introspection. She could feel her anger simmering below the surface, and if she wanted to avoid another outburst— which would result in two days of wearing a hair shirt for penance — she would do well to calm herself. She splashed freezing water from the washbasin onto her face. It was refreshing, but it only reminded her of the austerity she now faced daily. Already dressed in her postulant's dark gray gown, she'd tucked her roughly shorn hair beneath her wimple, and a large wooden cross hung around her neck. The undyed wool of the dress made her skin itch, and it chafed the open cuts upon her back. But it was far better than the hair shirt they forced her to wear the third day she arrived. She'd lashed out at another postulant who bumped into her as they entered their pew. The postulant was formerly a lesser noble, and Madeline reminded her that she, Madeline, was the sister of a laird and a former lady-in-waiting to Queen Elizabeth de Burgh. Madeline's voice carried, but the other woman was more discreet in her own set-down, as she pointed out that Madeline's brother was the one to banish her from court.

A Hellion at the Highland Court

An Angel at the Highland Court

A Harlot at the Highland Court

A Friend at the Highland Court

An Outsider at the Highland Court

A Devil at the Highland Court

THE CLAN SINCLAIR

His Highland Lass **BOOK 1 SNEAK PEEK**

She entered the great hall like a strong spring storm in the northern most Highlands. Tristan Mackay felt like he had been blown hither and yon. As the storm settled, she left him with the sweet scents of heather and lavender wafting towards him as she approached. She was not a classic beauty, tall and willowy like the women at court. Her face and form were not what legends were made of. But she held a unique appeal unlike any he had seen before. He could not take his eyes off of her long chestnut hair that had strands of fire and burnt copper running through them. Unlike the waves or curls he was used to, her hair was unusually straight and fine. It looked like a waterfall cascading down her back. While she was not tall, neither was she short. She had a figure that was meant for a man to grasp and hold onto, whether from the front or from behind. She had an aura of confidence and charm, but not arrogance or conceit like many good looking women he had met. She did not seem to know her own appeal. He could tell that she was many things, but one thing she was not was his.

> *His Bonnie Highland Temptation*
>
> *His Highland Prize*
>
> *His Highland Pledge*
>
> *His Highland Surprise*
>
> Their Highland Beginning

THE CLAN SINCLAIR LEGACY

Highland Lion **BOOK 1 SNEAK PEEK**

Liam Mackay gazed at the bustling Orcadian village of Skaill, on the isle of Rousay. He thought of how it reminded him of his clan's village, outside the walls of Castle Varrich in the Scottish Highlands. As he crossed the dock, he noticed the massive longboats that Norse traders sailed to conduct trade on the island. With his father's jet-black hair and emerald eyes, few would believe Liam had Nordic heritage, but it had connected his family to Orkney for ten generations. He swept his eyes over the crofts nearest the marina of sorts. He watched as a tall blonde woman stormed out of a house and slammed the door shut. The fury on the woman's face made him think of his mother when she was angry with Liam and his younger brothers and sister. But the woman before him, statuesque and voluptuous, couldn't resemble his petite brunette mother any less. Her tall stature belied her curves until she leaned forward to fill a bucket at the well.

"Elene, come back here. We are not through speaking," an older woman called from the doorway to the croft Elene Isbister left. The younger woman continued to fill the bucket as though no one spoke to her, but Liam watched her face grow red, and it wasn't from exertion. His path carried him toward the well, but he could have continued past to reach his destination. Instead, intrigued by the stunning blonde and the scene playing out before him, he stopped at the well as the woman finished raising the bucket. She poured the contents in her own pail before letting it drop back into the cavernous pit. Unaware of Liam, she jumped when he stepped forward and grasped the crank.

Liam's emerald eyes met deep sapphire, the shade of the Highland sky in autumn. Liam observed the surprise, then wariness, in her gaze as she stepped away. He drew the full bucket to the ledge and dipped the community ladle into the cool water. As he sipped, Elene took two steps back before turning away, disconcerted by the handsome stranger. However, her feet grew roots as the older woman stormed toward her. Liam kept his head down as he lowered the bucket, chiding himself for his nosiness but unwilling to move away. The older woman glanced at him dismissively before settling her attention on Elene.

In Norn, the language of Orkney, the woman continued her chastisement. "I didn't tell you that you could leave. We were in the middle of talking."

"No, Mother. You were in the middle of talking, and I was in the middle of not wanting to hear any more. I cannot believe you're considering marrying him."

"Not considering. I've already decided. When Gunter returns in a sennight, we will wed. Then we will all move home with him."

"Home?" Elene scoffed. "Norway hasn't been our people's home in ten generations. And you are a fool if you believe he will allow me to remain."

"You're old enough to marry."

"Getting married is a far sight different from being sold!" Elene made to step around her mother, but the older woman was just as quick.

"You exaggerate."

"And you believe a slave trader over your own daughter."

"Gunter is not a slave trader. You would smear his name because you aren't getting what you want, you selfish child."

Clearly not a child, Elene stood to her full height as she gazed at her mother, who was at least two inches shorter than her daughter. "Selfish," she repeated her mother. "I hadn't realized Katryne and Johan raised themselves."

"I am their mother."

"But I raised my brother and sister. I lost my chance to marry while you lost yourself in barrels of mead." Elene swung her glare at Liam, who'd remained near the arguing women while he spoke to his two ship captains. Despite speaking Gaelic, Liam sensed Elene knew he understood her conversation with her mother. It explained her accusatory glare.

"That was my grief."

Elene released a dismissive puff of air. "That was your habit. You haven't missed Father in years. You welcomed Petyre into our home almost every night, and Father hadn't been dead two moons."

"We need a man to provide for us," the older woman sniffed defensively.

Elene gawked at her mother before she laughed. "We do not need a man to provide for us. You might need one because you can't stand to be alone for more than a day. But I work our fields and hunt out supper. Petyre, and now Gunter, come into our home and eat the food I provide. I should have accepted Duncan's offer before he grew fed up with waiting."

"You didn't love him."

"You mean like you love Gunter?"

"I do love him," Elene's mother insisted.

"More fool are you," Elene muttered.

"Come inside. You're causing a scene."

"I'm not the one yelling. And I can't. I must bring Bess this water, feed the chickens, muck out the stalls, then milk Bess. I haven't time to argue when I know you refuse to believe me."

"He is not going to sell you!"

"He will. Or he'll force me to bed him. He will not feed and clothe another adult without getting something in return. He told me."

Highland Bear
Highland Jewel

Highland Rose
Highland Strength

PIRATES OF THE ISLES

The Blond Devil of the Sea **BOOK 1 SNEAK PEEK**

Caragh lifted her torch into the air as she made her way down the precarious Cornish cliffside. She made out the hulking shape of a ship, but the dead of night made it impossible to see who was there. She and the fishermen of Bedruthan Steps weren't expecting any shipments that night. But her younger brother Eddie, who stood watch at the entrance to their hiding place, had spotted the ship and signaled up to the village watchman, who alerted Caragh.

As her boot slid along the dirt and sand, she cursed having to carry the torch and wished she could have sunlight to guide her. She knew these cliffs well, and it was for that reason it was better that she moved slowly than stop moving once and for all. Caragh feared the light from her torch would carry out to the boat. Despite her efforts to keep the flame small, the solitary light would be a beacon.

When Caragh came to the final twist in the path before the sand, she snuffed out her torch and started to run to the cave where the main source of the village's income lay in hiding. She heard movement along the trail above her head and knew the local fishermen would soon join her on the beach. These men, both young and old, were strong from days spent pulling in the full trawling nets and hoisting the larger catches onto their boats. However, these men weren't well-trained swordsmen, and the fear of pirate raids was ever-present. Caragh feared that was who the villagers would face that night.

The Dark Heart of the Sea
The Red Drifter of the Sea
The Scarlet Blade of the Sea

www.ingramcontent.com/pod-product-compliance
Lightning Source LLC
LaVergne TN
LVHW031538060526
838200LV00056B/4558

9781648391286